LAST SUPPER

ALSO BY CHRISTOPHER CHARLES

The Exiled
Jonah Man (As Christopher Narozny)

LAST SUPPER

CHRISTOPHER CHARLES

ADAPTIVE BOOKS

AN IMPRINT OF ADAPTIVE STUDIOS | CULVER CITY, CA

Based on the original script by Jonathan Reiss

Visit us on the web at www.adaptivestudios.com

Library of Congress Cataloging-in-Publication Number:
2017960637

ISBN 978-1-945293-40-5
Ebook ISBN 978-1-945293-68-9

Printed in the United States of America.
Designed by Neuwirth & Associates.

Adaptive Books
3578 Hayden Avenue, Suite 6
Culver City, CA 90232

10 9 8 7 6 5 4 3 2 1

LAST SUPPER

· TEXAS, 2008 ·

CHAPTER 1

I t was one of those gorgeous-through-the-windshield Texas days, meaning the sky was pure blue, and so long as you had the air-conditioning cranked high, you didn't care that it was pushing a hundred outside with the air wet enough to drown you. The state was set to execute Joshua Slither, a serial killer with a church graveyard's worth of bodies on his résumé. Slither ground his victims up in an industrial meat grinder, which caused an evidentiary nightmare for law enforcement. What he did with the meat remains a matter of speculation.

After a good three hours of driving, I could see the Huntsville Unit of the Texas State Penitentiary cropping up on the horizon, looking like a medieval town where the walls and buildings are all made of the same dark-red brick. Stand back and look at the place long enough and you start to feel as if that single shade of red might drive you mad. During the Civil War, Huntsville put inmates to work stitching Confederate uniforms. After the war, it became the first desegregated institution in the state, an irony I can't imagine sits well with many black Texans.

The camera crew—three middle-aged men in indie rock T-shirts—was waiting at the gates to film my entrance. Every episode started with me driving through the prison gates in the brand-new BMW that I got for nothing from a local dealership. I asked the producers if it wouldn't be easier just to film me entering one time and play that under the credits for each episode, but they said it would create continuity issues on account of the weather and how I was dressed. Fine by me—I got a luxury car out of it, though in the end that became just one more thing for me to worry about losing.

I parked in my designated spot, and a corrections officer who looked like he regretted every minute of his life thus far led me and the camera geeks to Slither's cell. My job for this segment was to interview the inmate about all his best experiences with food. Truth be told, I'd have done just as well if they jotted down the name of his favorite dish on a scrap of paper, but the producers claimed the show would fall flat if the audience couldn't feel an emotional connection between me and what they called my clientele.

The CO opened the cell door, and the crew and I piled in. Slither barely looked at us. He both was and wasn't what I expected. Shaved head, no shirt, slathered in tats, wiry muscle from head to toe—all par for the course. But there was something deliberate and maybe even a little seductive about the way he avoided eye contact, the way he sat balanced on the edge of his cot in a cell cramped with equipment and bodies. He was the shy boy who taught himself to perform in public. If I had to guess, I'd say his victims liked him right up until the moment they became his victims.

But then the crew chief yelled "Action," and Slither looked me up and down like I was the meal instead of the chef.

"So you're the death row gourmet?" he said. "I pictured you small and kinda flimsy, but you must bench . . . what, two fifty? Two seventy-five?"

I shrugged.

"Yeah, you look like a real shitkicker," he said.

"I'm here to talk about you."

Slither smiled like he'd caught me in my first lie, which in a way he had.

"We all know why you're here," he said. "Baby brother's got himself a room one flight up."

This took me off guard, and Slither was quick to notice.

"Ain't no shame in it," he continued. "Funny, though, how Ryan McCallister's date with the needle keeps getting pushed back. That the deal you made? A gourmet stay? Still, you know the finale's coming, right? Can't stall forever. Hell, that's television I'd pay to see. Austin's top chef cooking his only brother's final meal. That's real human drama."

I thought of something an executive producer told me on day one: *They'll try to get under your skin, but remember, anything they say is fair game for the cutting room floor.*

"Let's start with the appetizer," I said.

"What's that, now?"

"The small dish before the meal. Like a salad, or a—"

"Skip it."

"Skip it?"

"Yeah, skip it. I never been fussy about food. Pretty much ate whatever anyone put in front of me, as long as it had some meat to it."

He stopped short of winking.

"All right," I said. "What about the main course? There must be some foods you like more than others."

"Why not just give me whatever it is you're gonna make your brother? Like a dry run."

"Maybe 'cause you're not my brother."

"No, I ain't," he said. "Hell, I don't know. You done this before. You tell me. What goes good with pentobarbital?"

He held his smile like one of those mimes at the mall. I almost felt sorry for him. I could see he was drawing out the interview because he liked the attention and was hoping to spend as few of his final moments alone as possible.

"Most people choose some kind of comfort food," I said. "Something that takes them back to their childhood."

He sniggered.

"My childhood's the last fucking place I'd go looking for comfort," he said. "And comfort's the last fucking thing I want."

"Now, that's hard to believe," I told him. "Everybody must want some comfort at the end."

"You a priest or a cook?"

"Cook."

"That's right. And who do you think's watched more people die? You or me?"

"You."

"Right again. And I ain't heard no one ask for comfort yet."

"So what did they ask for?"

"Nothing. Not a damn thing."

"Because they knew you wouldn't give them anything."

"You're wrong about that."

"Wrong how?"

"One hundred percent."

He sat up straight, leaned forward on his elbows.

"Let's play a game," he said. "Imagine I got you on the floor. Knee buried in your chest, knife to your neck. What is it you want?"

"I want to live."

"Too late for that. You've accepted as much. So now what is it you want?"

"I want it to be over."

"Wrong, wrong, wrong."

It was starting to feel like the school bully had his hooks in me.

"I give up," I said.

"Your own death's all you got left in this world, so you want it to last. You want to feel it, smell it, taste it. If you could, you'd watch. You'd study the agony on your own face. You want to be all the way there. No distractions. No worries. The way you've never been there before in your life."

The philosophical turn was a surprise.

"I can't give you any of that," I told him.

"Course you can't."

"Since I'm here, what do you want that I *can* give?"

"Well, now that you mention it . . ."

"Yeah?"

He went back to looking like he did when we first walked in: sheepish and kind of folding into himself.

"Before I go," he said, "I want to split my asshole taking one last shit on this world. I want to let loose, fill my drawers. We're talking whirly splats. Make it stink to high heaven. I want the grunts who carry me off that gurney to be haunted till the end of days."

I sat back on my metal stool, grinning wide.

"All right," I said. "Let's talk Texas chili."

CHAPTER 2

For the next segment, they filmed me shopping at a local market—a sprawling, Texas-sized emporium with a produce aisle as wide as a Paris boulevard. This was always my favorite part of the show, and maybe the only part, aside from the actual cooking, that I truly enjoyed. This was when I felt most alone. Not alone as in lonely, but as in free to explore my own thoughts. Because if there's one thing I've learned about being on TV, it's that the camera has no idea what anyone's thinking. I might appear to the viewer to be absolutely intent on what I'm doing—squeezing heads of lettuce, sniffing saltwater fish for that telltale odor of brine, checking the skin of a squash for bruises and scars—when really my mind is elsewhere, planning the week's specials for my restaurant, replaying last night's date with Cheryl, calculating what I'll owe in quarterly taxes. And that difference between what I seemed to be focused on and what I was actually thinking made for a sweet kind of solitude, like I was guarding the last bit of myself against thousands of prying eyes.

Once my basket was full of the ingredients to Slither's dinner and the cameras were turned off, I made a quick run back through the store, gathering what I'd need for Ryan's meal. I was going to make him the prix fixe I'd be offering at Companion all that week: Texas stuffed mushrooms glazed with steak sauce, a king ranch casserole featuring four cheeses and three kinds of meat, pecan pie sprinkled with sea salt and topped with Dutch chocolate ice cream. Because Slither was right: I'd made a deal with the warden. I'd host a cooking show that put a caring and compassionate face on a prison forever in the news for all the wrong reasons, and in exchange I'd get an evening per episode alone with my brother in one of Huntsville's conjugal apartments.

With the shopping done, we headed back to the prison, where the crew would film me cooking in the Alcove, an offshoot of Huntsville's main kitchen. The Alcove was built specifically for *Last Supper* and was modeled on my kitchen at Companion. It featured a stainless steel gas range with ten cast-iron burners, a Turbo Air reach-in three-section freezer, a thirty-gallon tilting kettle, a thirty-six-inch gas charbroiler with manual controls, and a fifteen-and-a-half-inch electric cast-iron crepe griddle. *Last Supper* gave viewers the impression that the Alcove was Huntsville's sole kitchen, but it wasn't large enough to serve a third of the prison's population and only a handful of carefully vetted inmates ever got near it.

They kept three cameras—two static and one handheld—trained on me while I prepared Slither's chili. At the producers' whim, I was decked out in a gourmet chef's outfit, complete with the kind of puffy white hat I'd never have been caught dead in at Companion. Mitch, who worked the handheld, zoomed in as I cut the beef chunk into three-quarter-inch cubes, then diced up the onions and tomatoes and garlic (in the pilot, they used slow-motion effects to highlight my knife work, but the result looked like an outtake from a low-budget kung fu film). Under normal circumstances, a single serving would have called for an ounce of guajillo chilies and another of pasilla chilies, but in honor of Slither's request I toasted two ounces of each. I threw in a few extra tablespoons of lard, too, and was unsparing with the red pepper. A Texas-style colonic if ever there was one. I only hoped that Slither's bowels could last until they strapped him down.

In the final edit, this segment would be rolled into a montage: snippets of me chopping and basting in my puffy hat spliced with footage inspired by Slither's life—a tracking shot of the street he grew up on, stills of the public school he attended, interviews with key figures from his childhood (a distraught mother, a sister who washed her hands of him long ago, a coach who either did or did not see this coming), followed by similar interviews of people close to his victims, most of them pissed off that Slither was getting a gourmet dinner out of the deal.

Originally, the producers wanted me to serve the inmate his meal, then sit with him in his cell while he ate. I refused. I wouldn't serve the meal, and I wouldn't be there to watch him die. I wasn't squeamish or sentimental, and Lord knows I'd seen people die before, but there's a difference between sentimentality and down-right mawkishness. The producers dug in, and it looked like there might not be a show at all until I proposed an alternate ending: have a loved one of the inmate's choosing sit with him while he ate his last bites.

The TV people were back on board, but now it was Ottie Woodrell, the warden, who took convincing. Having a civilian penetrate the inner sanctum of death row violated just about every rule in her book. Set that precedent, she claimed, and she'd be opening herself up to a flood of special requests—and nothing leads to litigation faster than a request denied. On top of which she feared alienating the public by appearing *overly* sympathetic: after all, did murderers like Slither offer their victims the chance to share a final meal with someone they loved?

At the end of the day, though, she came around—partially because she had a thing for me—and so my involvement in each episode ended with what I called the solemn handoff: the moment when I passed a silver tray loaded with my handiwork to the loved one, who would then be escorted by a team of COs to the inmate's cell.

Slither, who either abandoned his loved ones or saw his loved ones abandon him, hired a prostitute, or a woman I suspected of being a prostitute, though he called her a cousin *many times removed*, which I guess could be true of anyone. She was just under five feet, young without being pretty, and plump all over. She had blue streaks running through her black hair and wore two different shades of lipstick: violet up top and pink on the bottom. Her eyelashes jutted out a good three inches from her face, and her skirt was short enough that she'd have had trouble smuggling in contraband. She stood at the door to the Alcove, and the cameramen circled round while I carried her the tray.

"Obliged," she said, giving a little curtsy that she must've practiced ten times that morning. But then I'd practiced this part, too. I never knew what to say, and I always felt like the camera was burning right through me, so I made a little script for myself. Not word-for-word, but a general idea to work from. You couldn't say "sorry for your loss" because technically the inmate wasn't lost yet, and "sorry for your imminent loss" just sounds bad, so I skipped the sorry altogether and opted instead to highlight the kindness and strength of the loved one. I'd given myself three or four stock phrases to choose from, and with Slither's call girl I landed on *It's so good of you to do this. I know how hard it must be.* I could say that and have it ring true, since, as Slither highlighted, my own brother was waiting for the needle himself.

"Obliged," she said again, like maybe she was one of those foreign escorts and that was the only word of English she knew.

"I hope this meal gives him some small bit of happiness in his last hours," I said.

I handed over the tray, and right away her eyes started to water— not like she couldn't contain her sadness, but like the odor rising off my chili was sticking hot daggers in her eyes. I thought the smell alone might give her the runs, and I knew then that Slither would be satisfied with what I'd done.

"Obliged," she said again, and that was more or less the end of our interaction. I watched her walk off with a small troop of COs, and in my head I could hear the maudlin violins swirling the way they would on TV.

•

I changed back into my regular clothes, and that same droopy guard who met me in the morning led me over to the Huntsville conjugal apartment, where I had an hour to cook before they brought in Ryan. The apartment itself looked like the interior of a seventies-style mobile home. Where there wasn't wood paneling, there was the gaudiest flowered wallpaper you'd ever seen, and where there wasn't jaundice-yellow linoleum, there was mauve shag carpet. It was clean enough, though, and everything from the plumbing to the stovetop worked without a hitch.

I spread the ingredients over the counter space and got to prepping. I'd made the pie and stuffed the mushrooms the night before, so I didn't have much to do there, but I wanted the casserole to come out piping hot and fresh. I set the oven to 350 degrees and started the oil heating in the pan, and then it was off to the races. I'd made this dish so many times before, I didn't have to think much about it, and that gave me room to think about other things. Things I didn't necessarily want to be thinking about. Things that activated my sweat glands and made my heart throb like I had the hiccups in my chest. Mostly, I thought about all the times I'd done wrong by Ryan, or at least failed to do right by him. The kind of memories you want to shout out of your head. Like this one time before our parents' accident when I was maybe eleven and he couldn't have been more than six and I found a dead garter snake on the side of the road and all I could think to do was pick it up and mush it in his face. Or this other time when the Thompson twins were giving him a wedgie and instead of fighting them off I joined in. Stuff Ryan himself probably didn't remember, or maybe he did, but chances were he had my more recent transgressions on his mind.

The doorbell rang just like it was my own house, and then Ryan came strolling in, the guard having been kind enough to uncuff him outside. We're about the same height and about the same build, but the physical similarities stop there. There's no false modesty in my telling you that Ryan got all the looks in the family. I'm not saying my face would stop clocks, but if Ryan had been an actor or an athlete, he'd have been named *People* magazine's Sexiest Man Alive twice over by now. For a time, I was the kind of jealous you feel way down in your groin, but it's hard to keep that going into adulthood.

And so my jaw must have dropped a good mile when I ran up to greet him and saw that his matinee-idol face had been more or less rearranged. One eye had swelled up about five times the size of the other, there was a shiny purple lump on his forehead and a bare-knuckle gash cutting diagonally across one cheek, and his upper lip was like an awning hanging out over his chin. My first thought was that his good looks had gotten him into trouble, but that wasn't so likely with him locked away on death row. Besides which, Ryan knew how to handle himself.

"Goddamn, Ryan," I said. "You found yourself one hell of a beautician."

He held up a hand as if to say *no big deal*, but he knew he couldn't get off that easy.

"Sit your ass down and tell me what happened," I said, pointing to the Formica table set up in a space you might call the dining room or living room, depending on your mood.

"Just a new CO letting me know who's boss," he said.

"Well, what's that fucker's name?" I said. "I got some sway with the warden. I think the old gal even fancies me a bit. You want him transferred or fired?"

"Little late to start fighting my battles."

And there it was: that brotherly resentment, right on the surface.

"This isn't the playground," I told him. "When you're a grown-up, shit like this should have consequences."

"Not in here," he said. "In here, the consequences only come down on one side. Try to prove otherwise and you just make it worse."

It was hard as hell, but I managed to back off the subject for the sake of not spoiling his R & R.

"You hungry?" I asked.

"Always," he said.

"Then let's fill you up."

I fixed him a heaping plate of everything I'd prepared, including the pie. Ryan was always strange like that. If you didn't give him everything at once, he wouldn't eat anything at all. You had to give him broccoli to get him to eat his ice cream. Later, when I turned serious about my cooking, it drove me kind of nuts, because you couldn't get him to give an opinion on just one part of a dinner. Ask him if the meat was overdone and he'd say everything on his plate needed salt. But then if there's one thing you learn as a chef, it's that everybody's got to enjoy a meal in their own way.

While we ate, we talked about the heat and tried to remember the last time either of us saw snow. We debated whether any pitcher would ever get more strikeouts than Nolan Ryan and whether Clemens belonged in the Hall of Fame. We ranked the Star Wars films for maybe the thousandth time. Everything seemed kind of normal then, like we were sitting at some other table during some other time in our lives, a time we probably both took for granted. It wasn't until we'd finished eating that the conversation turned serious.

"You heard Cole is back in Austin, right?" Ryan said.

Jon Cole. That was a name neither of us had spoken out loud in a long while.

"Bullshit," I said. "He's less than a quarter of the way through a murder sentence."

"Yeah, well . . . his behavior must've been real good."

"He always could fake it when he had to."

There was a time in our childhood, not long after our parents' accident, when Cole looked like our savior. He ran a community center in North Austin, and it was a good place to be whenever our aunt tied one on, which was most days and all nights. Cole taught Ryan to box and let me have my way in the kitchen. He gave us somewhere to be and lots to do. But like they say, ain't shit for free, and Cole took plenty in return.

"Who told you?" I asked.

"New CO."

"Same one who did that to your face?"

Ryan nodded.

I lowered my voice to a whisper. "We need to handle this," I said.

"Consider it handled," he whispered back.

"How?"

"I'm gonna give that CO a cellblock vasectomy."

"Oh yeah, that'll solve everything."

"What can it hurt? I don't see them killing me twice."

"Keep your shit together and they won't kill you once. Cheryl's gonna—"

"Cheryl's a piece of ass, but she can't do shit for me. They got me dead to rights."

I didn't like him talking about Cheryl that way, but it wouldn't do for me to say so: he didn't know I was sleeping with his attorney, and Cheryl thought it best to leave him in the dark for now.

"She can keep the needle out of your arm," I said. "She's done it before, more than once."

"Even if she can, what's the point? Tell the truth now, James. You could either end it all in a minute or spend the rest of your life inside: which one do you choose?"

I leaned in real close and said, "I'd take living every time. You know I would."

We were quiet for a minute, and then we gave up talking altogether. I took out a deck of cards, and we played a few hands of 500 Rummy. It's not much of a game with just two people, but we were in it for the company. Ryan and I have always been best when we're quiet together.

It seemed like no time at all before the guard was back, knocking on the door.

"Yeah, all right," Ryan called.

He turned to me.

"Thanks for the food," he said, just like he always did, without telling me what he thought of it.

"I got something else for you," I said.

I dug into the freezer bag I'd carried his meal in and pulled out the latest issue of *Texas Rangers Magazine*. I never cared about baseball one way or another, but there was a long stretch when Ryan didn't care much about anything else. He didn't play, or even want to play. He wanted to be a broadcaster. He wanted to travel the country and see all the games. That's Ryan in a nutshell: always more interested in the side thing than the thing itself. The saddest part was, he'd never made it out of state, and now he never would.

"This is a special edition," I told him. "Check out the centerfold."

He kept flipping pages until the surprise fell out: a chunk of chocolate infused with one hundred milligrams of cannabis. One of the perks to hosting *Last Supper* was that with the cameras on me all the time, the guards didn't so much as pat me down. That was Woodrell's idea: keep the tone friendly and upbeat, even if I was cooking for dead men.

Ryan just about teared up with gratitude. There was nothing he liked better than feeling a little floaty at bedtime. He tore the tinfoil off and ate it right there, which was a safer bet than taking it back to his cell.

I winked. "Sleep tight, baby brother."

"No worries," he said. "Death row is about the quietest place on earth."

But I left there feeling like I had a whole lot more to worry about now than I did when the day started.

CHAPTER 3

And that's why, instead of going home, I headed straight to Companion, a place where I always felt a hundred pounds lighter, like I could just jump right off the earth if I wanted to.

It was going on eight o'clock when I left Huntsville, and the restaurant closed at eleven, but I made the three-hour drive in closer to two hours by throwing caution to the wind and clamping down real hard on my bladder. I got there around ten, which was perfect, because that last hour or so was always my favorite, especially on a weeknight. The crunch would be over, and the customers were down to regulars at the bar—most of them single retirees who liked to end the day with a bit of companionship—and people who'd decided to take life a little less seriously, at least for an evening. With closing in sight, the staff would start to get punch-drunk, which probably cost me in comped desserts and digestifs, but it was worth it just to sit in a room where everyone seemed at peace. Sometimes I'd look around and pinch myself, because Companion was exactly the restaurant I'd dreamed of owning since I picked up my first ladle—sleek and chic, with a menu that gave the food most Texans grew up loving my personal flare: brisket soaked in beer and crusted with brown sugar, chicken-fried steak prepared using slow-cooked bone broth and whole limes, blueberry cobbler made with almond flour and topped with lemon whipped cream, sweet tea flavored with agave. I even offered tofu fajitas for vegetarians, though they're a rare breed south of the Mississippi. Zagat was over the moon, and you'd have trouble finding a paper that didn't give Companion top billing in Austin, if not all of Texas.

That night, I parked in the back and entered through the kitchen. Maxine, my sous-chef, was busy preparing a last round of desserts while the rest of the crew broke down for the evening. Someone had ordered a banana flambé, which always made me nervous as hell with Maxine, because she poured the brandy on thick and had a habit I didn't much like of letting her ponytail hang down over one shoulder. But I figured she hadn't set herself on fire yet, and I wasn't in the mood for scolding.

"Any problems tonight, Maxine?" I asked.

"Not a one," she said. "Easy-peasy."

Which, true or not, was exactly what I'd hoped to hear. I pushed through the double doors and came out beside the bar, a long and elegant nineteenth-century mahogany number I rescued from a condemned hotel and restored to its original gleam. Max, who happened to be Maxine's twin brother, was pouring a tumbler of Jameson and jawing with one of the customers. He saw me standing there and fixed me a kir without even asking, which was his way of acknowledging where I'd been and what I'd been doing and who I'd seen afterward.

"Obliged, Max," I said, then half-grinned, realizing the phrase had come to me from Slither's whore friend. Slither, who was settling into the morgue right about now. I raised my glass to him and said a quiet little prayer. Chances were I'd never find out if the chili hit its mark.

I looked the restaurant over. We stopped seating at ten, and the bustle had just about trailed off. Another thing I liked about this hour: no one ever asked me for an autograph or tried to grill me about what it was like sitting face-to-face with killers who were themselves about to be killed. The regulars at the bar knew me and either we'd talked it through already or they couldn't care less, while the occasional customers were deep into their conversations by now. Best of all, there wasn't anybody milling around the front door, waiting for a table. The one fly in Companion's ointment was that people came at peak hours just to hobnob with the host of *Last Supper*. Most of them called the restaurant by the TV show's name, and probably none of them gave a fig about the quality of the food. Of course I couldn't complain about the steady traffic, but I guess you might say the clientele didn't always match the decor.

My heart was fluttering a little because I'd texted Cheryl and asked her to meet me for a nightcap. She hadn't texted back, but that usually meant she'd be there. I walked a wide arc around the bar, toward the two-seater I kept in perpetual reserve. Sure enough, there she was, sitting over a martini and chatting with Louis, my sort-of business partner—sort-of because he only served one role, and that was to explain how I managed the opening costs. Louis was an aging and well-respected local businessman who'd made his modest fortune in dry cleaning. When I opened Companion, roughly eighteen months earlier, I was a thirty-two-year-old line cook with a brother who'd just been arrested for robbery-homicide. No one would have believed I'd come up with the money by legit means. Of course, Louis didn't actually front a dime. Our deal was simple: his signature on the paperwork in exchange for bottomless meals and libations. But the restaurant was more than that to Louis, which isn't to say he went hungry: as a widower pushing eighty, Companion became his second home, or maybe his first home, because it was hard to imagine he did more than sleep and shower in his luxury condo.

Not that I'm complaining. Louis turned out to be a blessing, a kind of millionaire mascot who gave his age spots nicknames and told stories about a war I was pretty sure he'd been too young to fight in. A father figure, not just to me but to staff and customers, too. He was part of what brought the bar regulars back night after night. Maybe he made us all think it wouldn't be so bad at the end.

I was within a few feet of the table, and they still hadn't spotted me. Both of them looked relaxed, the way I hoped to feel soon, and maybe I did a little just seeing them. Cheryl was dressed casual, in jeans and a peach-colored sleeveless blouse, her black permed hair hanging just past her shoulders, and she was wearing the turquoise earrings I'd given her on our six-month anniversary. Louis was nursing a scotch, swirling the amber liquid around in his glass while he laughed hard at something Cheryl said.

"Sounds like you guys are maybe having a little too much fun," I told them.

"Well, that'll stop now that you're here," she said.

She didn't jump up to hug me, and I didn't lean over to kiss her, because we both agreed that discretion was in my brother's best interest.

"I was just keeping your seat warm," Louis said, standing. "As warm as I could with what blood I've got left in my veins."

"Didn't mean to chase you off," I said. "Sit with us for a while. I'll pull up a chair."

"Nah," Louis said. "I'd better get home and start trying to fall asleep. These days my bedtime routine lasts half the night."

"All right, then," I said.

"Sure you don't need a ride?" Cheryl asked.

"The night walk's part of the routine. That and a few hours of infomercials. Never thought I'd be developing new bad habits at my age."

"They aren't bad if they make you happy," Cheryl said.

"That's a slippery slope," he said. "But at least I haven't bought anything yet. Resisting is part of the fun. Makes me feel superior."

I watched him carry his glass over to the bar, then head for the door. From behind his age hardly showed, and I knew for a fact he could still knock out thirty push-ups. There wasn't a doubt in my mind he'd make a hundred.

"So how'd it go?" she asked.

"Which part?" I asked, taking Louis's seat.

"Let's start with the part where you saw my client."

"Well, I wish I could say he was in better spirits, though I guess they could be worse under the circumstances."

I decided against mentioning Ryan's makeover. Telling her about the new CO would be borderline pointless unless I told her about Cole, too, and telling her about Cole would lead to a whole deposition I didn't have the energy or will to give just then.

"I've got some news that might cheer him up," she said. "And you, too. I know how hard these days are for you."

She reached into her handbag and pulled out a manila folder labeled "David Green." Green was the plainclothes cop Ryan supposedly shot and killed.

"The firm's investigator dug up some choice stuff," she said. "Turns out Green had quite a history."

"Of?"

"'Cutting corners' would be an awfully nice way to put it. He was more or less pathologically incapable of identifying himself before he pulled his gun. Of course, most of the time that's a he said/he said, but the issue came up at a half-dozen different trials, so we can establish a pattern on appeal."

"Would that be enough?"

"By itself, probably not. But there's more. Detective Green was notoriously shoddy when it came to collecting evidence, and more than one of his witnesses cried coercion. He had two cases overturned in a single calendar year, and that same year he was suspended twice for excessive force."

"So how did he . . ."

"That's the real kicker: his uncle is the mayor's chief of staff."

"How did this not come up before?"

"The fuckers buried it. The mayor's office, the cops, and especially the DA. He knew that revealing Green's guardian uncle would open up a big can of mitigating circumstances."

"When you say they buried it—"

"Detective Green's record was mysteriously wiped clean after his death. We had to dig really deep."

"So Ryan has a chance?"

"At staying alive, yes. Maybe even freedom, though he'll be Louis's age before that happens."

"Freedom?"

That was so beyond anything I'd let myself hope for that it seemed far-fetched.

"If we play this right. We'll have to leverage what we know, offer to cover up the cover-up. Election season is just around the corner. The mayor won't want a whiff of this in the media. He barely eked out a win the first time around."

"In that case, can't we—"

She knew where I was going, and I guess just about anybody would have: I was practically rising out of my seat.

"James," she said, holding up a hand, "I'm against the death penalty. I'm against it in any and every case. That's why I work defense and not prosecution. But Ryan did what he did. I'm not looking for more than what's fair."

I hung my head a little, then forced a smile.

"You're right," I said. "Of course you're right. Still, sounds like a good reason to have another drink. You want one?"

"I better not," she said. "I've got court in the morning."

"So I guess you won't be coming over tonight?"

"Rain check."

"Then how about I walk you to your car?"

Cheryl drove an outsize Jeep with tinted windows, and we sat in it for a good while, listening to the hard rock station and necking like teenagers, and I had to confess to myself that I was in love with this woman. She was brilliant and beautiful, and she had a mean streak you could see from the moon. Not nasty mean, but bulldog mean: once Cheryl took up a fight there wasn't a whisper of quit in her. Every battle became a cause, and God help you if you stood in her way. That quality alone was enough to make her the most sought-after defense attorney in a state the size of France, and I felt pretty damn good having her in my corner. And yeah, in the back of my mind I was thinking maybe I could work her a little, get Ryan a decade or two of life worth living.

After she was gone, I headed back inside. The last of the customers was settling his bill. I had Max fix me another kir, then told him he could take off. I chased away the rest of the staff, too. Then I sat at the bar, drinking and listening to a jukebox full of western swing. There's something about being alone in a public place that makes life tingle in just the right way. Specially when it's a place you built. A place that wouldn't exist without you. And if you've never taken the time to bask just a little in whatever it is you like most about your life, then I recommend you do so just as soon as the opportunity arises, because Lord only knows what's waiting around the bend.

CHAPTER 4

Since I'd let the staff go early, there were still some dishes to be done and counters to be hosed down and other preparatory matters to attend to, none of which I attended to that night. So I was back at Companion before the sun came up, feeling a little hungover and not at all rested. I started with what was left to do in the main room, wiping down tables and sweeping up anything obvious enough to catch my eye. The bar was in good shape because Max always tidied as he went, so I headed into the kitchen and noticed straight off a bucket of leaf lard sitting open beside the stove, which is more or less an invitation to all brands of vermin. I slapped the lid back on the bucket and carried the bucket to the walk-in freezer, which I'd neglected to lock the night before. I must have been more tired than I realized, because I had to fumble around for the light switch, and then when I found it I damn near spontaneously combusted, because there was Louis sitting propped up against a shelf of pastry dough with the top of his head blown off.

Once I remembered how to breathe, I dropped the bucket and ran over to him like there might be some chance he was still alive. He wasn't, of course, so I just kind of fell back on my rear and watched the scene like I expected it to change, like Louis would bounce up and yell *April fools*, even if this was mid-July. Then I just kept shouting *no, no, no* again and again, which I understand isn't original, but that's what came out. It wasn't until I felt the cold again that I stood up and had a long look around.

It's hard to say now what I processed at the time and what I've added on with hindsight, but I know it wasn't long before I realized he wasn't the one who'd fired that pistol sitting on his lap. For starters, the trays behind and above him should have been covered in blood and brain matter, but they were so damn clean I could have cooked up the dough and served it without any problem at all. Second, I'd found the lights off in the kitchen and the freezer, but there wasn't a single thing overturned or knocked out of place. No way an eighty-year-old man with a generous helping of scotch in his veins groped his way through the restaurant without leaving a trace. Besides which, there would have been no reason for him not to turn the lights on, because if he was beyond wanting to live, I had to imagine he was beyond worrying about my electric bill. And then the way he was sitting, with his partial head hanging forward and his legs lying straight out in front of him, was just a little too posed, a little too pathetic. He'd been killed somewhere else, then placed here.

So I was skeptical even before I spotted the note stuffed in his blazer pocket, and though I was frozen with denial and closer to a heart attack than I'd like to admit, I at least had the presence of mind to fetch a pair of latex gloves before I touched anything on or near Louis's person. Once I had the letter out and unfolded, I sat right there in the freezer and read it, not even noticing the cold:

Dear James:

I hate that my good run is ending on a bad note. I thought I had it in me to be a party to murder, but I was wrong. For a while I debated going to the authorities, turning myself in, and letting them know how Companion came to be. But despite myself, I've grown fond of you—too fond to make you pay for your (our) transgressions. I only hope that your deal with the devil does not destroy you, the way such deals most often do.

My wife's death gutted me, and I let myself be seduced by the idea of a project to carry me through my final years. That project is tainted; I no longer have the stomach for it, and I feel it is time to join my beloved.

This world was fun while it lasted. I don't much care what you do with my body.

Goodbye—
Louis Avery

Even in my shocked state, I knew this letter was 90 percent bullshit, and there was no way in hell Louis wrote it. The facts as stated were true enough, but the sentiment was all wrong. Louis never had the slightest doubt he'd done the right thing in fronting for me. Companion gave him a new lease on life. If anything, he was too damn grateful, and there were times I wished he'd shut up about it.

Then there was the letter itself: typed in block letters on plain-Jane white paper. Louis was a product of his era. If he had something to say, no matter how minor or major, he wrote it by hand on thick, cream-colored stationery. Even more telling: he never once in the almost two years I knew him said "my wife." He always called her Roberta, like using her title would be claiming some kind of ownership over her. In fact, for a long time I wondered if they were ever married at all.

But the real giveaway was that Louis never knew—or, as far as I could tell, even suspected—the reason behind our arrangement. I'd gone out of my way to keep that from him. I told him I'd won the money during a trip to Vegas. In fact, I did more than tell him. One of Ryan's less sketchy acquaintances managed a casino on the strip, and I paid him ten grand to vouch for me by phone and on letterhead. I convinced Louis that the police would never let the brother of a cop killer open his own business with his own money. They'd find some way to cry foul. They'd shutter Companion's doors before it ever opened. And they'd seize every dime. But Louis was a pillar of the community. He'd donated large sums to Police Athletic League and the public library and Big Brothers Big Sisters and just about every charity that ever staked a claim in Austin. No way they'd take him on.

All in all, Louis's death was about the worst staged suicide in the history of murder, so much so that whoever killed him wanted me to know the suicide was a sham. And I had no doubt who that someone was. Ryan hadn't been talking out the side of his mouth: Cole was back in Austin, walking around loose. This was a message, and I responded exactly the way Cole wanted me to: I panicked.

I panicked because whether or not it was ruled a suicide, my partner's violent death would bring the cops running. They thought my brother had killed one of their own, and if they had a way to ruin his kin, they sure as shit wouldn't pass it up. That was the not-so-veiled threat in Cole's forgery. If all he wanted was straight-up revenge, it could just as well have been me sitting in Louis's place. No, Cole was angling for something deeper, and until I knew what that something was, I had to erase any tracks he made as best I could. Having my brother beaten and my partner killed was just his way of saying he had something worse in store for me. He wanted me to feel the hellfire coming from every direction.

I decided right then and there that I'd counter his first move by making Louis disappear. Louis's life had been an open book for anyone at Companion to read, and every regular knew that his favorite place on earth was Buenos Aires. His Spanish sounded a lot like English to me, but he was fluent enough to carry on with any native speaker who wandered into the restaurant, and he was always joking that the reason he'd stayed with Roberta for five decades was that he'd never found a better tango partner. So why not send him to Argentina? I fished down in his front pocket, pulled out his wallet with my gloved fingers, and flipped through the laminate windows until I came up with a platinum credit card. In no time at all, I'd bought him a one-way ticket to the Paris of South America from the office computer, which would make sense to the cops given that on paper he was half owner.

The next part was a whole lot less pleasant and involved about a half dozen industrial garbage bags, two of which I cut holes in and draped over my own body like a double poncho. I didn't cut him up, if that's what you're thinking, but it was no small feat getting his torso in one bag and his legs in another, then wrapping him up with the rest and tying the whole package tight with a six-strand twine that cut right through the latex gloves and into my palms. Ideally, it would've been a two-person job, maybe three, and I wasn't firing at full capacity to begin with. And if you're picturing Louis as some frail octogenarian you could pick your teeth with, then I'm here to tell you you're dead wrong. He was six foot something and weighed a good 220, and my feet kept slipping on a frozen patch of fish broth that someone, probably Maxine, had neglected to clean up.

Luckily it was still dark out, and there was no one around to see me drop a man-size parcel from the loading dock into the trunk of my car. With that done, I came back and bleached the hell out of the freezer. I couldn't really spot much blood, but I figured it had to be there, seeping into cracks and crevices and generally eluding the naked eye. Then I drove out into the desert and buried him in a construction site I'd read had been shut down due to safety violations.

The digging was hard work, but it gave me some time to reflect, even if my reflections were scattered and pulling me in different directions. On the one hand, I couldn't stop imagining Louis's death, or maybe the last hour or so of his life, with Cole standing over him, prodding him with a pistol, telling him everything would be okay if he just signed. I wondered if Louis resisted, and if so, for how long. I didn't see any bruises or rope burns or anything to say he'd been tortured, but then Cole needed a pretty corpse to make the suicide look legit. I was glad for that much, but still Louis's last moments couldn't have been any seaside stroll, and that was damn hard to take because Louis, in all the time I'd known him, had never said an unkind word to anyone, not even in passing. Maybe he was one of those guys who'd been a prick early on and then softened in his waning years, but old-man Louis would bend over backward to make you feel like your life was pure sunshine and you'd be a fool to trade places with anyone. Part of me wanted to find Cole right then and make sure he suffered more than Louis had. I wanted to see him cower and bleed and beg, and then I wanted to be the one denying him mercy.

On the other hand, and almost at the same time, I was trying to work out my own path to safety, because, like I said, whatever Cole had done to Louis, he had worse in store for me. He already had me

standing out in the middle of the desert in broad daylight commit-
ting a felony. Maybe he wanted me behind bars, where he could come
at me whenever it suited him, the way he'd come at Ryan. If that was
true, I felt just a little better knowing that while folks at Companion
might get curious about Louis's sudden absence, there wouldn't really
be anybody to investigate. I felt like he'd done me a personal favor by
not having kids. True, I'd taken his age into account when I picked
him—my silent partner couldn't be young and ambitious, and he
couldn't have *too* long to live—but I hadn't thought much past that.
It was a blessing to know there wouldn't be anyone scrambling after
an inheritance. Hell, if I picked up his mail and canceled his utilities,
there might not be any kind of investigation at all. At least not for
a long while, and even then they'd find that plane ticket and think
Buenos Aires was the sunset Louis chose to ride off into. *Yes, sir,* I told
myself, *you did good work here.* Which I know might sound insensitive
given the circumstances, like maybe I wasn't really that broken up
about Louis's departure, but I was in self-preservation mode. I loved
the man. I did. He was the closest thing to a father figure to come
along since Cole. I felt awful about the part I'd played in his exit,
and I knew I'd feel a whole lot worse once my innards settled down.

The question right then was, *What next?* Because say what you
want about Cole, but he'd never been one to hatch a partial plan.

CHAPTER 5

I'd put in a full day already, and the day before hadn't been any picnic, either. A normal person might have called Maxine in to cover for him, but the kitchen's always been my safe place. I guess that's true for most people who have found their calling. A runner loses himself on the track; a musician forgets all about taxes and death while he's taking his solo. It was the same for me with cooking, straight from the start. Dump a pile of raw ingredients in front of me and right away I see the final meal taking shape; I know exactly what a dish will taste like just from the way it smells. I'm gifted, but I don't mean that the way people usually do. The gift isn't talent—if anything, talent is the curse. It's the talent that separates you from other people. The gift comes in being able to immerse yourself so deep into something that the whole world drops away.

So when I was done at the construction site, I headed straight back to Companion. The waitstaff had mostly arrived, which meant the early lunch customers wouldn't be far behind. I hired direct out of UT—college kids whose world-at-my-feet attitude usually gave me an energy boost, but today their faces were a little too fresh, a little too eager. I smiled and nodded my way through them, then headed to the bathroom to wash the dirt from my fingernails. The cool water felt good, and for a while I just sat on the edge of the toilet and let the faucet empty onto my wrists. Then, despite myself, I went back into the freezer for a final inspection. The bleach smell was stronger than I would have liked, and the cement floor was a shade lighter in the area where Louis had sat, but there was nothing to say that I'd found a man with his top blown off leaning against the pastry shelves that morning. That was between me and Cole.

Once I'd finished puttering, I slipped on my apron and fired up the stove. I don't know if it was the morning's trauma or the lack of sleep or the mere fact that Cole was back, but in that dead spell before the first order came in, I found myself reliving the first time I ever cooked for someone else.

•

That someone was Ryan. I must have been twelve, which would have made him seven. In my mind, it was the very night our parents died, but that can't be right because I remember it was still light out and they were killed at 9:45 p.m. in the middle of winter. A church bus full of senior citizens headed home from an Indian casino in New Mexico hit a patch of black ice and skidded head-on into their Chevy Cavalier. It was over for them instantly, but for me and Ryan everything was just beginning.

Our mother's sister took us in, in part because the state agreed to give her foster money. I guess Aunt Joan looked good enough on paper—she worked the register at a local Kmart and owned her three-room shack outright—but she was a fall-down drunk and junkie with a rattlesnake's temper, and our mother hadn't had a thing to do with her for years. In fact, the night Aunt Joan brought us home was the first time I'd seen her place, and I can't say I was impressed. Not that Ryan and I were accustomed to luxury—Dad was a mechanic and Mom worked part-time at a multiplex concession stand—but they kept a clean home and did everything the right way. Early to bed, early to rise. Three square meals. Prayers at bedtime. American, salt-of-the-earth values through and through.

Aunt Joan, on the other hand, crawled through life without a plan or purpose. Any effort she made went into drinking and drugging herself to death, and if it wasn't for her job, she'd have been a pure-bred shut-in. Her idea of cleaning was to throw things at the garbage can and hope they landed. Your skin clung to anything you touched, and you couldn't get from one room to the next without sidestepping between columns of boxes she'd never unpacked in the twenty years she'd lived there. The cat was obese from gorging on mice. If something broke and couldn't be fixed with duct tape, she just let it lie. Plug in the toaster and the TV shut off. Run the shower and the kitchen sink at the same time and the basement would flood. The floorboards were warped and splintering to where you couldn't walk in your bare feet. There were car parts in the front yard, which I never understood 'cause she didn't have a car or even a license.

Most days her shift ended at three, and she'd start drinking vodka from a water bottle the second those automated doors shut behind her. By the time she reached the end of the parking lot, she'd popped a few pills and snorted a line.

Like I said, I remember it as our first night there, but that can't be right, though I'm sure it wasn't long after. She'd passed out on the sofa where Ryan and I were supposed to sleep. Ryan was crying a downpour, and I couldn't find any way to make him stop. I stood over her, pushing on her shoulder, but she wouldn't budge. Part of me wondered why she was alive and our parents dead. Part of me, even at that young age, thought it would be as easy as pinching her nose shut and clamping a hand over her mouth. But then what would happen to me and Ryan? Aunt Joan was the devil we knew, and at least she mostly ignored us.

Meanwhile, Ryan's bawling was working my last nerve, and I couldn't get him to stand more than three inches away from me. It took everything I had not to test my backhand on his jaw.

"Ryan," I said, "what is it, buddy? You're gonna dry yourself out crying like that."

He didn't answer on the first go-around, but eventually I got it out of him: he was hungry. And then I realized I was hungry, too. We'd had dry cereal for breakfast and nothing since. My first thought was to dig through Aunt Joan's purse until I came up with enough loose change for a pair of Big Macs, but it was dark out and I didn't know how to walk to the strip mall from there.

"Let's see what we've got," I said.

I took his arm and yanked him into the kitchen, though I knew he would have followed me anyway. The pantry was overly large for a six-hundred-square-foot home—maybe as big as the kitchen itself— but Aunt Joan hadn't exactly stocked for the apocalypse: all I found were some dented cans of lima beans I figured she'd stolen from a food drive at work.

I turned to the refrigerator, which was dripping with duct tape. Duct tape on the handles, duct tape on the door hinges, duct tape holding the magnetic gasket in place. Inside, the vegetable drawers were missing, the light was out, and the bottom shelves were coated with a thick brown gelatin. There was food to be had, though. Not a lot, but some. There were two egg cartons with three eggs apiece, a container of heavy cream, a fat chunk of mossy cheese, an unopened jar of pickles, and enough sticks of butter to stock a supermarket for a week. Of course, the cream had turned ages ago, but the eggs looked solid, and the pickles might have been brought home that day.

The freezer was the real treasure trove, because packed in around vodka bottles of varying sizes were unopened bags of strawberries and blueberries and blackberries and raspberries and just about any other berry you could name, like one day at the store she'd had a short-lived epiphany about getting her health on track.

I poked around in the drawers and cabinets, seeing what kinds of implements there were to cook with. Aunt Joan had a butcher knife and some butter knives and nothing in between. Most of the forks had tines missing, and the spoons all had that tarnished, oil-slick coloring to them. Aunt Joan's only frying pan was in good shape, though—probably because she never used it.

Meanwhile, Ryan's crying had sputtered out, and he even seemed a little curious about what I was up to. I started to take the eggs and butter out of the fridge, then realized there wasn't anywhere to put them. The only counter was piled high with empty pizza boxes and takeout containers and bottles of pop and cans of beer.

"Oh well," I said, sticking the eggs and butter back where I'd found them. "I guess we'll just have to make room."

I gestured for Ryan to stand aside, then used both my arms to set the whole mess airborne—boxes and bottles and tins flying in all directions, bouncing off walls and cabinets, and coming to rest on the floor in a series of crashes that would have woken anyone in the world but Aunt Joan. Ryan was tickled. He started laughing so hard his tear ducts were churning again, and I was laughing right beside him, happy to have stumbled onto something that flipped his switch. But then he stopped short, went pale, and just kind of pointed.

Turns out I'd disturbed a Roman Empire–sized colony of roaches, and they were scurrying over one another trying to find new cover. I'd never seen so many in one place. Some were babies and some were the size of a Saint Bernard's paw. I waited for Ryan's scream, but he was more fascinated than afraid. He walked right up to the counter and stuck his face an inch from the action. Then he raised one hand high over his head, like he'd smite them all with his bare palm.

I pulled him back.

"I got a better idea," I said.

We took turns putting the frying pan to good use. Ryan focused in like he'd found his true calling. He even got playful with it, dragging the pan to smear the corpses and make blood-and-guts designs on the counter. I guess I should have known then that there was something different about him, but I just figured he was blowing off steam he'd kept bottled up for too long, and Lord knows we both had enough of that.

It took what felt like an hour to get the space cleared out, and by then the air in Ryan's stomach was making a racket I could hear from across the room. I sat him down on a footstool and got to work. I'd watched my mother make omelets plenty of times. She'd break the eggs into a red plastic mixing bowl, then add cheese and ham and spinach and mushrooms and let me beat the whole mess with a whisk while she melted three pads of butter on the frying pan.

I couldn't find a mixing bowl or a whisk in Aunt Joan's kitchen, and she didn't have any ham or vegetables, so I improvised. I lined up three cereal bowls on the counter, broke two eggs into each, and threw the shells into the sink, where every once in a while a stray cockroach would stick its head out of the drain. Next, I took up the cheese and cut away the moss and sliced what was left into uneven cubes. I dropped a handful of cubes into each bowl, then fetched the bags of berries from the freezer. I cut a small hole in the top of each bag, sprinkled blueberries in one bowl, raspberries in another, and blackberries in the third.

Just like Mom did with me, I put Ryan in charge of the beating while I melted butter in the pan. I gave him a fork with three tines, showed him what to do with his wrist, and told him not to spill any. He was as careful as a seven-year-old could be, but there was yolk clinging to the outside of every bowl when he finished, and I couldn't stop him from licking the fork.

It all cooked up in no time, and I didn't have any trouble with the eggs sticking to the pan. For extra flavoring, I drizzled packets of soy sauce over the top and knocked the last of the salt out of its shaker, then garnished the whole thing with slices of pickle. And there was my first creation: a cheese, mixed-berry, and pickle omelet. It didn't look like much or have any particular odor, but Ryan eyed it like it was his own mini birthday cake.

We took the pan and two forks out into the front yard and crouched down on a rusted bumper and ate the whole thing in under a minute. Afterward, Ryan initiated a belching contest, and I was happy to let him win. I was happy—period, because those deformed and freakish omelets gave us our first hint that life might be good again.

•

I stood at the stove, sautéing pork and onions for a double order of Texas crepes, and couldn't remember a thing about how that omelet tasted more than two decades ago, only that as I was making it I thought, *This is me. This is what I'm supposed to do.* And now, so many years later, I tried thinking the same thing again—*This is me. This is what I do*—but the words didn't hold, didn't seem to have any meaning. I felt about a million miles from *me*, whoever that was, and for the first time on record I couldn't find any pleasure in cooking. My mind was somewhere else, trying to make sense of life's big-ticket items while my hands worked by rote, and that had never been true before. Cooking was always the time when the world did make sense. Or else it was the time when nothing had to make sense, when the question itself was moot.

I told myself not to worry about it. Today wasn't like other days. I hadn't woken up expecting to find Louis dead in the restaurant freezer. Anybody would be on edge.

That feeling will come back, I thought. *It'll be there tomorrow, and the day after that.*

But I was a long way from convinced.

CHAPTER 6

I t didn't take long for Cole to put in an appearance. I was supposed to spend that night with Cheryl, but by the time the lunch crowd was back to work I could barely hold my eyes open. I was happy to get her voice mail when I called, because just talking was more effort than I cared to make, and I wasn't keen to share the particulars of my day. Instead, I told her I'd caught a stomach bug and was planning to wait it out in bed.

So I made the short drive back to my condo with every intention of sleeping myself into oblivion. I was so damn eager to shut my eyes that my legs started shaking with anticipation while I was waiting for the elevator, and then I could barely get the key in my front door. Soon as I stepped inside, I caught a whiff of the tangerine sea bass I'd made for Cheryl maybe three nights ago, but I didn't think anything of it because with the windows shut and the central air on it wasn't unusual for smells to stick around.

I started the shower running, stripped to my boxers, then headed into the kitchen to make a cup of lemon-hibiscus tea, a beverage I don't much care for, but it helps me sleep. Back when I bought the place, I'd had the wall separating the kitchen and living room knocked out for entertaining purposes, and I was standing at the sink with the kettle in my hand when I spotted him: Cole, sitting stock-still in my striped recliner, like he was posing for a portrait. I didn't jump or startle or do any kind of double take. I just went right ahead and filled the kettle like there wasn't a reason in the world to alter my plans.

"Mind if I smoke?" he asked, pulling a cigar from his breast pocket.

"Suit yourself," I said. "Want some tea?"

He shook his head. There were dirty dishes and an empty ice cream container on the coffee table in front of him. He'd helped himself to what was left of that bass and polished it off with the last of my rocky road.

"Guess I should turn that shower off," I said. "And maybe put my clothes back on."

"Better not," he said. "I have a feeling that piece you carry is hanging on the back of the bathroom door. At least now I know you're not concealing."

I lingered for a beat, just kind of taking him in and processing our reunion. The blinds were drawn, and sitting there in the near dark, this older Cole looked to me like a nicotine stain come to life. His skin was puckered and yellow, his crew cut had gone all-the-way gray, and his pecs looked more like tits under his signature black V-neck T-shirt. He was one of those men who start to resemble a woman as they age, and that gave me no small satisfaction. Still, it was never Cole's physique that scared folks.

Once I'd finished sizing him up, my first thought was, *He must have been prepared to sit like that till rigor mortis set in, just to make an impression.* Because even I didn't know when or if I'd be home most days. My second thought had to do with killing him, but the .358 on his lap held me in check.

I pulled a decorative blanket from the back of the couch and wrapped it around my waist. The fish smell was buried in a cherry-scented smoke that I knew would still be reminding me of Cole's visit three days out. I sat on the couch and fixed him with a look that said, *Well, what the fuck do you want?*

"This is a really nice place," he said. "Really nice. You've come up in the world since the last time I saw you."

"Guess we've been traveling opposite paths."

Antagonizing him probably wasn't the sharpest move, but my filter was set to zero just then, and I couldn't stop wishing it was him in that freezer and Louis sitting here now.

"How long has it been?" he asked.

"Not long enough," I said. "You ought to have about a hundred years left on your sentence. The state of Texas must be going soft."

"I wouldn't count on it," he said, which was his way of letting me know we'd get to Ryan soon enough.

"So why are you out? A jailbreak would've made the news."

"Look at me. Do I look like a threat to anyone?"

"That revolver on your lap could do some damage."

"I'm too weak to protect myself any other way."

"Bullshit. Maybe I should give your parole officer a call. Report you for breaking and entering. And armed robbery."

"Robbery?"

"You ate my food."

"Nonsense."

"You wanna give me his name, or do I have to track him down?"

"It's a she, actually, and I'm afraid you'd crush her. She seems to have adopted me as a kind of father figure."

"I could tell her a few things about that, too."

"Yes, we all have things we could tell. By the way, how is Ryan doing? I heard he got into a scrape."

"Heard from who?"

"*Whom.* You've overcome the birth lottery in so many ways, but your speech always did betray you."

Fifteen years earlier, that *birth lottery* dig would have sent me spiraling, and I didn't like it much now, either, but I couldn't let him know it. I didn't want him thinking he knew me at all anymore.

"You're right," I said. "I should make more of an effort. Heard from whom?"

He grinned.

"I had dinner at Companion last night," he said. "While you were away filming. I was sitting alone at the bar, and this lovely older gentleman took it upon himself to join me. Your partner, as it turns out. I have to admit, I was a little piqued. I guess I considered myself irreplaceable."

He must have thought he had me, but I wouldn't bite. He'd have to be the one to place Louis in my freezer.

"What did the two of you talk about?"

"Dry cleaning, at first. I never knew a man could be so animated and tedious at the same time. But things picked up when I steered the conversation toward you."

"What did he say?"

"Oh, he gave you all the credit in the world. Said you were the brains and talent behind the operation. Called himself a pseudo-restaurateur. I didn't tell him that you and I were old friends."

He was grinning now, like he could put me in checkmate at any time but didn't want the game to end. I was just waiting to hear his demands.

"Still, your friend Louis wasn't entirely happy, was he? Something about dubious circumstances surrounding the opening of your restaurant. He wouldn't go into detail, at least not then, but I could sense guilt. And loneliness, too. A rather profound loneliness. I suppose that's inevitable at his age. Especially for the childless."

That gave me an opening I couldn't let pass.

"How is your son, by the way? You two patch things up?"

I was pretty sure they hadn't or I wouldn't have asked the question. Cole went quiet for a minute. I couldn't tell if he was mad at me for hitting a sore spot or mad at himself for walking into the slight.

"My son has his life, and I have mine," he said. "Still, blood has a way of winning out in the end."

I shrugged. I didn't want to push too hard until I knew what he had planned.

"Back to your partner," he continued. "He must have sensed that I was a kindred spirit. Getting out of prison after a lengthy sentence is a lot like growing old. I don't mean end-of-middle-age old, like me, but the-end-is-in-sight old, like Louis. The world looks very different than it used to. The people you knew a decade ago have all moved on. As an ex-con, you find your so-called friends suddenly unavailable; as an old man, you find them dead. So I wasn't surprised that we hit it off. I wasn't surprised that he would confide in a stranger, since the world, at this stage, has no one else to offer him."

"He talks to me," I said, careful to use the present tense.

"Ah, but you're so young, at least by comparison. And you have the stink of business on you. A man can only say so much to the arbiter of his fortune. Especially when that person is also the cause of his unhappiness."

"Me? I didn't cause anything."

"Don't be so modest. You've always exerted a stronger influence on people than you realize."

"Maybe, but I think you're way off on this one. Yeah, Louis misses his wife, but the guy loves being alive. I mean, his resting face is a smile. And he did damn well for himself. Companion is just pocket change."

"Maybe you're right. Maybe I'm overreacting. Maybe his paranoia is just a symptom of old age—one that comes and goes and leaves no lasting mark."

I was supposed to ask what Cole was overreacting to. I was supposed to ask about Louis's paranoia. Instead I just sat there.

"I have to admit," he went on, "that I let myself get a bit inebriated last night. I haven't been out that long, and I guess I'm still in a celebratory mood. Anyway, this morning, I woke up and couldn't quite remember how Louis and I parted. I had a vague sense that we'd made plans to see each other again, but I couldn't remember a time or place, and when I went through my phone and wallet I found no sign that we'd swapped information. So imagine my surprise when I went to fetch the paper and found a package from a Louis Avery resting against my door."

"A package?"

"A manila envelope, hand-delivered."

He reached behind him and pulled the envelope in question out of a back pocket.

"From a man you'd only just met?"

He nodded.

"It's not like you to go around handing out your address. I guess you must have been very surprised."

I was hamming it up, of course, but he wasn't about to let my tone put a damper on his little show.

"The contents were quite concerning, so I thought I should bring them to your attention."

"Bless your heart."

He kept on ignoring me. He pulled a letter from the manila envelope, unfolded it, and slid on a pair of reading glasses.

"*Dear Mr. Cole,*" he started.

I thought I knew what was coming. I figured it had to be a carbon copy of the letter I'd taken off Louis that morning. I was as wrong as I'd ever been.

"*It will seem odd that I'm sharing this with a man I only just met, but I don't know many people anymore, and I guess you're freshest on my mind. That, and you seem like a good sort. I'm writing to you because I believe my life is in danger.*"

Right there my mind made its adjustment, and then I really did know what was coming. I thought about charging him, making a play for his gun, but Cole would have prepared for that. There'd be other copies addressed and ready to go should anything happen to him. As long as I knew him, he'd seen every contingency coming. Except maybe for the day they locked him up, and even that he turned to his advantage.

"*I have reason to believe that James McCallister, my partner in Companion, is going to kill me. I've served my purpose, or rather his purpose, and now I'm one of only two people who know his secret, and the other is sure to be dead soon enough.*"

Cole was enjoying his recital. Of course, the writing didn't sound a damn thing like Louis—even in print he tended to curse like a sailor, and he never in his life called anyone "a good sort"—but that was past mattering now. Like I said, I knew what was coming, and sure enough it came. The letter laid it all out in vague but mostly accurate terms: how Ryan robbed and killed a drug dealer (Cole's nephew), then later killed a cop, and how I used the robbery money to open a restaurant with Louis acting as front man.

Cole's forgery may not have been worth much, but his guesswork was at least plausible enough to have *Last Supper* end with a real ironic twist. My leg was getting jumpy, and I could feel the sweat beading up along my hairline, but I still wasn't ready to concede anything just yet.

"Sent me a letter, too," I said. "Claimed he was running off to Buenos Aires. He honeymooned there with his wife. Said he needed a beautiful spot to die in. Who knows how many letters he's sent to how many people. He's old. He gets confused. I'll talk to him tonight."

"Oh, the time for talking is over," Cole said. "As you well know."

"What I know is—"

"Save yourself the embarrassment," he cut me off, brandishing the letter. "As soon as I read this, I ran right over to the restaurant, hoping to find you there. I'm an early riser. It's a hard habit to break after a decade in prison."

He lifted his eyebrows as though inviting me to finish the story for him. I declined.

"I saw you," he said.

"Saw me?"

"I saw you dump what could only be a human form into the trunk of your car. And then I followed you."

He reached back into the envelope and pulled out a sheaf of paper. He handed the pages over to me.

"See for yourself," he said.

There was one time-stamped snapshot per page, printed on the same generic white paper as the note I'd found in the freezer. The first page showed me standing on the loading dock, teetering under the weight of Louis's Glad-bagged body. Then came a series of my car traveling the interstate, one photo per exit, framed so that the license plate and the sign for the off-ramp were both clearly visible. For the finale, there were candids of me taking bolt cutters to the padlocked gate, driving onto the condemned site, digging a Louis-sized hole, dumping Louis into that hole and filling it back up, and tagging a porta-potty with gang-style graffiti to give authorities a reason for the busted padlock.

Stupid, stupid, stupid. I thought I'd been so careful. I'd scanned my surroundings at every stage, kept my eyes half-glued to the rearview mirror. At that hour, there hadn't been more than a trickle of cars on the highway, and I'd buried Louis in the most secluded spot I could find, way off behind a stack of steel piping they'd just left there when the site shut down. I couldn't figure how I'd been so damn sloppy, or where the sixtysomething, half-broken-looking Cole who'd emerged from prison had been hiding himself. Unless he'd hired some high-end private eye, but that was unlikely: Cole had always been borderline paranoid about limiting his tracks.

I must have looked all-the-way beat, because his voice turned almost gentle as he finished the kill.

"This isn't the only copy Louis left on my doorstep," he said. "There are six more in total, each addressed to a different recipient. The district attorney, the attorney general, the chief of police, two journalists, and one television anchor. I'm supposed to mail them in the event of foul play. For now, they're still sitting on my kitchen table."

"You're playing a dangerous game," I told him.

"This is no game," he said. "And the danger is all on your side."

"Are you sure about that? You and I both know what really happened."

"Yes, we do. You and your brother killed my nephew and stole my money."

"Ryan did that by himself. And he's paying the highest possible price."

"Oh, please. Ryan is half-wit muscle at best. I don't doubt he pulled the trigger, but the boy never had an idea in his life. But he would have followed you anywhere. I can't imagine his feeble little mind grappling with the betrayal. It's sad, really."

I saw myself lunging, grabbing the gun, training the barrel on his abdomen, and squeezing. I must have been telegraphing my thoughts, because he took the revolver up and thumbed at the trigger.

"Why not just ask for whatever it is you want?" I said.

He smiled like things were finally getting good. I sat back and waited.

CHAPTER 7

"Because I want to own you," he said. "And I'm pretty sure you'll never give that voluntarily. It's lucky for you that I've had so long to think. If I'd been out when you and Ryan murdered my nephew, you'd both be dead. Of course, the state has robbed me of the pleasure of executing Ryan myself, but they've given me the perhaps greater pleasure of watching his protracted death from afar. He must be so, so unhappy."

"He is. You have your revenge. I told you, I wasn't involved. Ryan's hated you for a long time. If you'd been out, it's you he would have killed."

I wasn't throwing Ryan under the bus; I was stalling, hoping Cole would talk long enough to reveal some new weakness. Ryan was an old weakness. Cole had always wanted more than my brother could give.

"Let's be clear," he said. "Your brother means nothing to me. He was born out of his depth, and this is about the best end he could have hoped for. My nephew was no great prize, either, but that doesn't mean I'm prepared to look the other way. As far as he and Ryan are concerned, this isn't revenge so much as housekeeping. No, you were always the prize, James. It's you who has to suffer now."

"I can almost understand that," I said. "But why come at me this way? Why kill an old man?"

"But I didn't kill him; you did. Still, I can't say that I'll mourn his loss. Maybe if he'd said a bit less about how he looked on you as a son . . ."

"I'll ask again," I said. "What do you want?"

"I'm getting to that. It isn't just that I lost my nephew: that money he was carrying was mine."

"It was drug money."

"It was my drug money, and I always wondered what happened to it. For a while I assumed the police pocketed it when they caught up with Ryan, but Louis was kind enough to fill me in. Once he explained his role in your venture, I understood immediately. So it seems Companion is mine. It was paid for with my money, no?"

"No," I said. "Not a chance. You can't come back after all this time and—"

He held up a hand.

"Don't worry, it's not your restaurant I'm after, though I may ask for the occasional meal, and I will want to conduct business there from time to time; it's a classy place, designed to impress the right kind of people. But I've got other ideas about how you can pay me back. And keep your brother alive and safe, at least for the time being."

There was a world of difference between what I was thinking and what I said: "I guess I'm in no position to negotiate."

"No, that's true. But then you may not want to negotiate once you hear what I'm proposing."

"Which is?"

"I've got some lost years to make up for. Some lost revenue. You're going to pay me back in trade."

"I thought you didn't want the restaurant."

"I'm thinking more about your television show. I've caught the last few episodes. You look so reluctant and hangdog at the outset, but then the inmate wins you over every time. It's like they're finding the humanity in you, instead of the other way around. It's compelling—some might say heartbreaking. Your talents are wasted on local cable."

You don't know real terror until the devil pays you a compliment.

"You want to be my manager?"

"Something like that."

He laid it out. We were going to take *Last Supper* national, hit every state with the death penalty, and broadcast from coast to coast. He already had a producer lined up. Probably a cokehead looking for a steady source of free blow.

"I can't do it," I said.

"We've been over this. You're in no position—"

"I don't travel well."

"But it will only be for a few days at a time. And who knows what it might lead to. You might get offers in New York or Los Angeles. You always coveted the big time."

"I was a kid then," I said. "I'm good where I am."

"Don't be so provincial."

"I have obligations here."

"You're objecting before you've heard the best part."

I gave him a look that said *go ahead*. He leaned back, crossed his legs, and balanced the gun on his top knee.

"It's a proposition that encompasses your full skill set," he said.

Bottom line: he wanted me to smuggle heroin into the prisons on his list, which included Huntsville.

"Like I said, I've seen your show. It was the credits that gave me the idea, the way they let you just waltz in. I imagine that's part of the publicity stunt: Huntsville took a long and well-deserved beating in the media. It must warm your heart to know that you're putting a compassionate spin on the institution that will kill your brother. They must have won back some of their funding already, which will help us argue for the same freedoms elsewhere."

"I'm out of that game," I said. "I have been for a long time."

"Oh, it's like riding a bike. Besides, you won't ever touch the stuff. All you have to do is drop the car at a garage and pick it up later the same morning. I'm offering you plausible deniability."

"If I refuse?"

"You won't. The more you think about it, the more you'll see that the advantages are all yours. I've taken care of everything for you. My CO friend will even babysit Ryan while you're away."

He picked up Louis's fake letter and waved it around.

"Consider the alternative," he said.

And then he got up and walked out.

•

I spent all that night considering. I couldn't imagine myself going along with Cole's scheme, but I couldn't imagine a way out of it, either. He'd put me in check with just a handful of moves, and all I could do now was stall and hope. Of course, he'd made those moves before I even knew I was playing, but that didn't keep me from second-guessing and more or less hating myself. I'd steered Louis into danger without giving him the full range of facts. He was a kind man who deserved a better end, and I doubled down on the self-hatred remembering all the times I was short with him, all the times I'd found myself bristling at his stories, just itching all over to get away because when it came to talking Louis could hold a sprinter's pace for the length of two marathons.

I tried to comfort myself by thinking maybe he'd been spared something worse.

Maybe cancer was lurking around the corner. Or Alzheimer's. With a little effort, I convinced myself I'd seen the signs already. Louis was forgetful as hell, and more than once I'd caught him talking to thin air. At least Cole's way was quick. And then, I told myself, I'd given Louis a reason to get out of bed when he most needed one. Without Companion, he would have been a sad and solitary widower these last few years. At least he'd had a final burst of happiness.

Of course none of that had anything to do with why I'd enlisted him in the first place, and the fact that I was sitting here in my loft-like apartment sipping overpriced gin and trying to make myself feel better while Louis lay cold in the ground spoke volumes about who I'd let myself become.

But then there wasn't much time to worry about my character. I'd botched things bad, and I had half a mind to use the Buenos Aires ticket myself. On the face of it, I'd taken about the dumbest route possible. I mean, I'd gone and implicated myself in a murder that might have passed for suicide. I guess most men will dig themselves in deeper if there's the slightest chance they might not face any consequences at all. Cole must have banked on that when he stuck Louis in my freezer. He understood how much I had to lose. He knew that Louis's violent death would put Companion in jeopardy and send me scrabbling. He knew I had a life worth fighting for and a brother I couldn't leave in the lurch.

But how did he know exactly what I'd do? How did he know to be waiting there with a camera? I'll admit, that part had me feeling really small, because like I said, Cole didn't go to any great pains overestimating me.

It was three in the morning by the time I thought to look at a clock. With all I had on my mind, curing cancer would have been easier than falling asleep. I swallowed a Flexeril and mixed myself an eight-ounce screwdriver, then turned on the TV and watched the infomercials scroll by, just like Louis would have done. Still, I couldn't stop thinking. I figured I had two options: come partway clean, or come all the way clean.

Partway clean would mean telling the cops how I'd found Louis and panicked and taken it upon myself to make him disappear. I'd have to leave Louis's fake suicide note out of it, for obvious reasons, which would mean an open investigation with me as the only suspect, and even if they managed not to find me guilty of murder, I'd still be facing a slew of charges. And then Cole could seal my coffin shut with a quick trip to the post office. He wouldn't have to implicate himself at all, wouldn't have to testify or even talk to anyone. That was the real beauty of his scheme. I mean, what could I do? Even the partial truth would mean confessing to about a dozen felonies, and it'd look like a premeditated insanity defense if I said Cole killed Louis so that he could blackmail me into taking my death row cooking show on the road.

No, there just wasn't any sense in coming partway clean. Besides which, Cole could get to me and Ryan both in prison. He'd made that good and clear.

The second option—coming all or at least most of the way clean—would mean exposing Louis as my front man and admitting that I'd opened Companion with Ryan's robbery-homicide money. My life would for all intents and purposes be over, but at least I'd know what the future held, and I'd have a good chance of taking Cole down with me. And a full confession gives you a sliver of bargaining power. I might be able to have Cheryl negotiate a few things before they sent me away. She might even be able to get protection for Ryan. Unless she cut ties with me altogether, which would be well within her rights.

To be honest, I didn't spend a whole lot of time pondering the all-the-way-clean option. Once the thing you care most about is at stake, you're pretty much willing to go ahead and risk it all. Especially when the potential upside is slight at best and far from guaranteed. No, until I hit on a solid plan, all I could do was play my hand and hope that Cole found a way to screw up worse than I had.

Meanwhile, I'd have to make sure that I kept Cole happy. If I could make him believe I regretted our rift and wanted more than anything to play nice again, so much the better. That might sound impossible just from the little bit I've said already, but Cole's big weakness is that he needs to be worshipped. He's as crafty and cunning and ruthless as they come, but grovel a little, say you'd be shit without him, and he'll believe just about whatever comes out of your mouth next. He'll move heaven and hell on your behalf as long as you stroke his ego. I wished to God I'd kept that in mind when he was sitting here in front of me.

But at least I hadn't given him a firm no. I hadn't told him to do his worst, to go ahead and kill me right there if he wanted. Because if there's one word Cole won't stand for, it's *no*, and if there's one thing he's good at, it's doing his worst.

CHAPTER 8

As you've probably gathered by now, running a community center was just a small part of what Cole did back in the day. He also ran drugs and numbers and what he called specialty sex workers—ladies who'd do just about anything a wife wouldn't. But it was a while before Ryan and I knew any of that, and by then we'd already been hooked. That was Cole's MO: find the kids who are raising themselves, give them a place to be and something to do, keep reminding them what their lives would be like without you, then offer the right ones a job. I was one of the right ones. He brought Ryan along because we were a package deal.

The center itself wasn't much to look at from the outside. It sat on the northern limits of town, between the last on-ramp to the interstate and a defunct set of train tracks. The ball field out back was just a diamond of lumpy dirt, and the building looked like a strip mall that people kept adding on to in different-colored brick. Inside, though, was another story. It was the inside Cole cared about. *State-of-the-art* would be an exaggeration, but everything—from the kiln in the crafts room to the medicine balls in the gymnasium—was sturdy and well maintained, and the pool was kept up to the swankiest health club's standards.

There was a cafeteria with a full staff, but they cleared out between meals, and then Cole gave me free run of the kitchen as long as he got to eat some of what I made. Not right away, but after Ryan and I had become more or less fixtures. And that might be what pushed me over the top as a chef, because I was always afraid that if Cole didn't like my cooking he'd cut me off, and then I'd have to keep using Aunt Joan's kitchen, making due with what little she pilfered from the grocery aisle at work, where they didn't sell a single vegetable and the meat and fish all came in cans.

Austin Rec was a full community center in the sense that it wasn't just for kids: there were odd night classes for adults, too. Not odd like strange, but odd like the catalog offered whatever local folks felt qualified to teach. Cole gave me what he called an honors pass, meaning as long as I didn't make a nuisance of myself I could sit in on any course I wanted regardless of age range. I tried my hand at juggling, learned to play a few chords on the guitar, and got as far as purple belt in judo. And of course I took every cooking seminar the place offered.

Cole kept Ryan on a shorter leash. From day one, he steered Ryan toward boxing, and he never let him veer off course. He claimed he saw Ryan's limitations early on, but looking back I'd say those limitations were awfully convenient for Cole. He was trying something new: grooming a kid for one purpose and one purpose only. Ryan was Cole's bodyguard of the future. Cole was in his midforties then and looking ahead to the time when he couldn't guard himself. Who better to protect you than someone you've trained since childhood?

Which isn't to say that Cole didn't have plans for me. Cole was all about the long term. I was going to be management of some kind. Maybe I was the kid who'd inherit it all, since his own son wanted nothing to do with him.

We'd been turning up daily for a couple of years before Cole brought us all the way into the fold. It started out innocent enough. He took me into his office—the ugliest room you've ever seen: fake wood paneling, drop ceiling, paper-thin green carpeting—and asked how I'd like to get paid for cooking a big shot's dinner.

"A senator," he said, "who wants to be governor. He's hoping I'll back him. I'm hoping he'll kick some funds our way. I'd like to add a music room to this place. Maybe a music wing, with a little theater where kids can put on recitals. Instruments, teachers, additional space—all of that costs money."

I was too surprised to do anything but nod.

"In other words," Cole said, "I need to impress this man. I need *you* to impress him. You'll be the shining symbol of all the good work we do here. Our gourmet prodigy. Capisce?"

I nodded some more. It took everything I had not to do a 360 on the swivel chair I was sitting in. I was all of fourteen, going on fifteen, and you'd have thought he was awarding me a Nobel Prize. The fastest way to a kid's heart—maybe to anyone's heart—is to offer him cash for something he'd do even if there was no such thing as money. For me that something was cooking. Put a spatula in my hand and the world disappeared around me. Questions about why my parents had to die and why I was born in the first place dropped away. In that sense, cooking's the only pure experience I've ever known.

So I guess you could say I owe Cole a lot. Hell, you might say I owe him everything. But when is a relationship ever that simple? The best con men all know that you have to give before you can take.

"Just tell me what to make, and I'll make it better than anyone," I promised.

Cole thought it over.

"Would you know what to do with a trout?" he asked.

I told him I did, though I'd never actually cooked one before.

"I read somewhere that the senator is a gold-medal fly fisherman," Cole said. "I never knew you could medal in killing fish, but then I grew up in a real city."

Already my mind was filing back through everything I'd learned in class and on my own. I was seeing capers and curlicue lemon rinds and parsley and tiny brown potatoes. I wanted to get started right then.

"What about dessert?" I asked.

Cole shrugged.

"His last name could be French. There's nothing I love more than lemon mousse."

"I like that," I said, mostly just to say something. It sounds crazy now, but my heart was racing.

"Excellent," Cole said. "I'll give them a tour of the facility, crack open a bottle or two of wine, and then you fix us all a nice meal. It'll be me, the senator, and his campaign manager. And make some extra for you and Ryan to eat on the side."

"You mean Ryan can come?"

"I think he should get used to being your helper. Don't you agree?"

"Yes, sir," I said.

He smiled.

"It's set for this Friday. Come here directly after school, like always. We'll go shopping together."

"I'll think through what I need," I said.

"Good boy."

I started for the door. He called me back.

"James," he said, "be prepared to listen, when you're not cooking. There will be some wheeling and dealing at this dinner. It's about time you got a taste of how the world works."

"Yes, sir," I said.

•

That Friday, I wore the nicest outfit I had: a beige cardigan with leather patches on the elbows, and black corduroy pants that were just a little faded at the knees. I decked Ryan out in a button-down paisley shirt, tucked deep inside a pair of white jeans—never mind that it was late May and most of the kids at school had their short sleeves rolled up to their shoulders. Pride is more important than weather. So it didn't bother me much when a three-time senior called us Salvation Army rejects. Normally I'd have taken my best-aimed snap kick at his sack, but that day I just laughed it off. I laughed off everything until the final bell rang.

Cole drove us in his Porsche to the sort of gourmet shop where you can't go wrong no matter what you buy. I knew there were specialty stores around Austin, but I'd never been to one, and though the sawdust on the floor confused me, I couldn't get over how the smell of the place changed every few feet: dark-roasted coffee followed by bitter chocolate followed by cheese sharp enough to make your eyes water. A little farther down, the meat department smelled like the fancy sausages you cut up and put on little crackers. Ryan hated that smell and pinched his nose, but I'd have stripped naked and rolled around in the display case if they'd let me.

They stuck the seafood section far in the back, probably because there's only one way fish smell, and it's not the kind of smell you want to greet people with. Still, I was struck by how many kinds of fish there are in the world, and just how colorful they all are, especially when the light hits their scales a certain way. I remember thinking that if fish smelled like chocolate, the oceans would have been emptied a long time ago.

After we'd wandered around for a bit, I handed Cole my shopping list and it was off to the races. For someone who didn't cook, he sure knew that store like the back of his hand. He took me straight from the dill to the almonds, and from the almonds to the lemon zest. He let me pick the trout myself and didn't argue when I told the man at the counter to leave the heads and tails intact.

On our way out, I had a sad moment thinking how my aunt lived just a few miles north but chose to eat out of cans and bags or not eat at all and just drink herself to sleep. I knew if she was there with us, she'd have pointed to a price tag and said there wasn't any choice about it, but at fourteen you have to believe people make their own way. They may not choose the track they start on, but after a while they choose whether or not to stay on it. There was a better life to be had, but Aunt Joan had given up and was more or less living out her suicide.

But my fit of empathy didn't last long. By the time we got back to Austin Rec, it would have shocked me to learn I even had an aunt. My head was deep in the game. Of course I knew this was all some kind of test, and I was scared witless at the outset, but once I sliced into that first lemon and a bit of juice sprayed onto my hand, I forgot I was cooking for anyone but me. That's always been true. When the apron goes on, the nerves switch off.

CHAPTER 9

C ole had me and Ryan set the table in a small dining room off
the kitchen, behind a door that had always been locked before.
I thought senators were royalty, so the shabbiness of the space
surprised me. There were no windows, the table had napkins stuffed
under one leg to keep it balanced, the wood floor was unvarnished,
the chairs didn't match, the chandelier hung from exposed electrical
wires, and a single unframed poster advertising a rodeo from the
1940s was all the decoration. I guess Cole saw me looking around
and read my expression.

"Whether you want money from someone or someone wants
money from you," he said, "it's always best to look like you don't
have much."

A little pang of self-doubt hit me then, and I thought, *That's why
you hired a kid instead of a real cook.*

I had the mousse in the refrigerator and the fish ready to hit the
pan before the guests showed up. One look at the senator and I realized I must have been off base about the stature of his profession.
He reminded me of a substitute teacher who can't get his students
to take their seats or stop talking or listen to a word he says, the
type you'd swear has mustard on his tie even when he doesn't. His

curse was that his face had no symmetry to it. He had dark bags under both eyes, but one of those bags was puffy and swollen, while the other hung withered like a popped water blister. The moles on his forehead were all clustered to the left, his chin looked like two mismatching half chins, and one ear jutted way out, while the other looked like it had been stapled to his skull. On top of which, it must have been a while since he checked his comb-over in the mirror, because his few remaining strands of hair had fallen off to the side under the weight of whatever pomade he was using, and the exposed scalp was peeling badly.

His manager, on the other hand, gave me a warped idea of what a campaign manager does, because even then I knew straight off he was muscle. He had that bleached and square-jawed Scandinavian look, and his big-and-tall suit was so snug you could just about see his veins through the fabric. He barely spoke, even when spoken to, and I figured he'd built himself up to compensate for the fact that no one cared what he had to say.

I tossed the salad and fired up the burners while Cole gave them a tour and Ryan tagged along. They must have stopped at Cole's desk for a whiskey or two, because I could smell it on everyone but Ryan when they got back. The senator had tugged the knot loose on his tie and seemed generally more relaxed, while the campaign manager looked like if he shut his eyes he'd be good until morning. Cole uncorked a bottle of wine and had Ryan fill the glasses, then called for me to start the food coming.

I was more anxious than scared, although I was scared, too. The questions wouldn't stop coming. What if someone choked on a trout bone? What if they found the potatoes overcooked or under-cooked? Should I have used butter instead of olive oil? Would the mousse be chilled in time? It felt like everything depended on this one night, like if I blew it I'd never cook again for anyone but Ryan.

Cole had instructed us to hang back and watch when we weren't in the kitchen or serving. If a glass was empty we were supposed to fill it. If a plate was clean we were supposed to clear it. What we weren't supposed to do was talk. We couldn't ask questions, and we couldn't join in the conversation. *A real chef is silent, invisible*, Cole had said. *He watches and holds still, communicates without words.* So when we weren't working, Ryan and I stood like columns in opposite corners of the room, waiting for someone to look needy.

And that waiting was the hardest part.

Ryan and I carried out the salads, then listened while they talked about the price of gas and Phil Niekro's knuckleball and anything but what they were eating. I studied their faces for some kind of feedback. No one puckered up. No one pushed their plate to the side or spat food into their napkin. I watched the campaign manager pick out the tangerines and dump salt on the spinach, but I couldn't find any lesson to be learned from that.

When they were about half done, I snuck back into the kitchen and started heating up the fish. Cole had a second bottle of wine open and half poured before Ryan and I brought out the main course. The senator spoke to me directly for the first time. He was able to name all the ingredients I'd used on the fish just by sticking his nose in the air and sniffing hard.

"Lemon, thyme, oregano, and of course garlic," he said. "And a touch of white wine."

"Cooking wine," I said, like he might bust me for serving alcohol underage.

"There are only so many things you can do with a flounder or a trout," he said. "What matters is how you combine those things. What you include, and what you leave out."

My anxiety must have shown on my face, because he went ahead and took a bite without breaking eye contact.

"Very nice," he said. "Perfectly balanced. And the flesh is like butter. I once caught a thirty-pound rainbow. I'd love to see what you could have done with him."

Well, my first impartial review was in, and as far as I was concerned, the evening could have ended right there. It didn't bother me a bit that the manager was just kind of pushing the potatoes around with his knife.

"I told you," Cole said, "the boy is gifted. That's what we do here at Austin Rec: we foster the gifted. Give them a place to practice and improve."

The senator downed another forkful.

"Yes, indeed," he said, still addressing me. "I may just have to take you along to the governor's mansion."

They went back to talking about nothing in particular, and I tuned out for a while, thinking maybe he really would take me to the governor's mansion. I wondered about all the dignitaries I'd cook for and what my room would look like and if he'd let me bring Ryan. And I wondered where I'd go from there. To the White House, maybe. Or maybe abroad. An American chef in Paris. Probably that had never happened before.

But then the tone of the conversation changed, and I tuned back in.

"So what do you say?" Cole asked. "Do you think you'll be able to siphon some of that state funding my way?"

The senator looked surprised, like he'd thought this was just a friendly visit.

"You want to get down to business, then?" he said. "Why not send the boys away so we can talk more freely?"

"I'm not sure that would be fair to them," Cole said. "Their imaginations will just run wild. They're sure to come up with things you and I would never dream of."

The senator's smile looked like the placeholder for where a real smile might go.

"Suit yourself," he said. "You should know, though, that I don't intend to pull any punches."

"Punches?"

"You can ply me with liquor and play man of the people all you want, but I know who you are and what you do."

"Is that so?"

"It is. Mind you, as long as you're compliant, I don't anticipate any difficulties."

"Compliant?"

"We can work together, on my terms, or we can work against one another, also on my terms."

Cole laughed out loud.

"Now, Senator," he said, "you didn't think this through very well, did you?"

"My thinking is fine."

"Maybe you just need an outside perspective. Take a moment to consider. If I wanted something from you, do you think I'd dress up in a suit and tie and come calling at the Capitol?"

"I find that hard to picture."

"Of course I wouldn't, because that's your world. It would be presumptuous of me to believe I could best you there. I'd have no sense of the parameters, no sense of what you could do to me, how you might come at me. Yet here you are, in my backyard, thinking you can beat me at my own game. You don't know the rules. You don't know what I might do, how I might come at you."

"At home or abroad, I have greater means at my disposal."

"That's arrogant, Senator. Very arrogant."

"I really think you should tell the children to leave."

"And I really think they should see this. Like me, they come from nothing. They need a lesson in how to handle predators."

"You're calling me a predator?"

"You're here to extort me, aren't you? I'm trying, in your best interest, to offer you an alternative. I'll back your play for governor. All you have to do in exchange is direct a grant or two my way. You're in this for personal gain. I'm in it for a music room."

"I work for the citizens of Texas," the senator said. "Let's throw all our cards on the table, shall we? You're a drug dealer. I won't funnel a dime into your pocket."

"But you'd have me buy your way to the governor's mansion?"

Cole let the question hang there, then turned to face me and Ryan.

"I want you to pay attention now," he said. "This is how the haves keep the have-nots away from their pie."

"I know exactly what you're doing," the senator said. "You're using these boys as witnesses. That's clever. Cynical, but clever. But so far all they've witnessed is *you* threatening *me*. And all you've done is raise the stakes. And maybe ruin my appetite, which is a damn shame, because this meal really is exceptional."

He stopped being angry at Cole long enough to give me a wink.

"I'm afraid we'll be going now," he said, starting to rise. "Thank you, boys, for your hospitality."

Cole reached across the table, put a hand on the senator's wrist.

"Not until you've made your proposition," he said. "I promised these boys they'd leave here tonight with a greater understanding of how the world works."

The senator nodded at his campaign manager, who I couldn't help but notice was sweating all over his forehead.

"Like I said," the senator told Cole, "even on your terms, even in your backyard, I have the upper hand."

Cole looked at the campaign manager. The campaign manager didn't look back.

"Your boss stays," Cole said, "but you can leave now if you want to. That's an offer I won't make twice."

The campaign manager got to his feet about as slowly as a man could stand. He started to reach inside his blazer, but before he found what he was reaching for, he had Cole's fork lodged in his jewel sack. The high-pitched squeal undid any fear factor that came with his physique. He doubled over, dropped to the floor. Cole, without getting up from his chair, leaned down and fished a blackjack from the man's inside blazer pocket.

"That's it?" he asked. "No gun?"

He looked almost amused as he finished patting the manager down.

"I'll be damned," he said. "You just have no idea, do you? But maybe you're starting to figure it out?"

"What do you want?" the senator asked.

"I want you to sit down and tell these boys exactly who I am, and exactly why you came here tonight."

"I have to get this man to a hospital before he bleeds out."

"Then I suggest you talk fast."

The senator took his seat, opened his mouth to address Cole.

"No, no, no," Cole said. "You talk to them, not me."

The senator shifted in his chair, folded his hands on the table. He looked at Ryan, then thought better of it and locked eyes with me.

I have to hand it to him: he wasn't scared; it was pure hatred that had his voice quaking. Chances are you've already figured out the broad strokes of what he told us, but there were details I never would have guessed. Cole came to Austin by way of Philadelphia, where he grew up in foster care. He was bright enough to get a full ride to the Wharton School of Business, a place I'd never heard of before, though he quit after just one semester.

"I found better ways to make money," Cole said.

"More expedient ways," the senator said. "It's hard to see how they're better."

From what I could gather, Cole started out selling painkillers to the elderly through someone who worked for a chain of retirement homes. The administration got suspicious, so Cole took his business to the street, expanding it to include coke and heroin. The young Cole was ambitious and prone to mistakes, and it wasn't long before the competition drove him into exile.

"Legend has it that he threw a dart at a map and hit Austin," the senator said.

"Well, that's true," Cole said, "but only on the third try. I wasn't about to live in Duluth or Slant Rock."

The manager, still writhing in a fetal position on the floor, unleashed a long groan, and Cole kicked him hard for it.

"Go on," he told the senator. "You're getting to the best part."

Whether or not he chose Austin at random, Cole found the place to his liking. The smaller market suited him. He lay low for a while, did some recon, then started knocking off drug dealers like a niche serial killer. There was zero risk of retaliation because nobody knew who the fuck he was. Cole made himself the big fish in no time at all. And once he had the narcotics game nailed down, he branched out into gambling and whores.

"And some legitimate businesses," the senator told me. "Like Austin Rec. Though those are just a front to make his money appear clean. He's a drug dealer, a pimp, a murderer, a loan shark. He's a sociopath. The more people suffer to line his pockets, the better he sleeps at night."

Cole smiled.

"Well, there you have it, boys," he said. "A factually accurate account, though I'd argue that the good statesman here has certain things ass-backward."

"Which things?" the senator asked.

"To begin with, Austin Rec isn't the cover-up; it's the cause. As you yourself pointed out, I spent my childhood bouncing from one foster home to the next. Austin Rec was the goal all along. It's a place where kids know they're safe and cared for. A place where they're valued. A place where they're taught to value themselves. I give them everything their parents should but don't. I save souls here. You can't change the world if you play by the rules. You must know that or you wouldn't have come to me."

"So you poison one generation to save another?"

"I'm practical that way. The truth is, adults are beyond saving. But not children. Never children."

The manager, having figured out that no one would come to his rescue, decided now would be a good time to try and get up. Cole knelt beside him, grabbed a fistful of his hair in one hand, and pummeled his face with the other. The senator started to lunge across the table, then thought better of it. Ryan just stood staring the way he'd stared at those cockroaches. The manager flailed his arms as Cole busted his nose and shattered his cheekbones and caused both his eyes to swell shut before he finally lost consciousness.

Sometimes, on long drives or in bed at night, I still wonder if Cole spiked the manager's wine. There were other possibilities. Maybe that man was no more a bodyguard than he was a campaign manager. Maybe he was the senator's steroidal cousin who thought he'd make a few easy bucks that night. Whatever the scenario, watching Cole make short work of a guy who would have blended in on the Cowboys' front line left an impression.

When he was done, Cole popped back up, lay his bloody hand on the table, and studied it like he was trying to figure out what went wrong. Then his eyes shot back over to the senator.

"Now, tell me again what it is you wanted?" he said.

The senator looked about ready to give back my trout.

"Nothing," he said. "I don't want anything."

"Then I guess it's time to talk about what I want."

The senator nodded. He hadn't looked like much to begin with, but he was top-to-bottom diminished now. "It's clear to me that the state has been negligent in its support of Austin Rec," he said, staring down at his near-empty plate. "If elected, correcting this oversight will be my top priority."

Cole smiled.

"Then you've got my vote, Senator," he said. "And I just can't wait to cast it. I know this night didn't go the way you planned, but I hope you learned something. I really do. Stay within yourself, Senator, and I have no doubt you'll achieve great things."

"I need to call an ambulance now. Please," the senator said.

"I'm afraid that might attract the wrong kind of attention. But we've got a dolly lying around here someplace, and we'll help you get him to the car. It's up to you if you see him all the way to the ER or just drop him at the curb. He's a little inebriated, so no one will doubt he found a way to cause this. If I were you, I'd volunteer as few details as possible."

It wasn't until years later that I understood the real purpose of that evening. Cole had been putting on a show for me and Ryan. There were easier ways to resolve his conflict with the senator, but this was the finale to our recruitment. This was Cole letting us in. And from that night forward, we were either in or out.

This might sound strange, but discovering who he really was hit us harder than our parents' death. We thought of him as our personal savior. Imagine you met Jesus Christ one night when you were still young and impressionable and instead of turning the other cheek or walking on water he decided to drown Pontius Pilate right in front of you. Just held his head underwater until he stopped breathing. You'd be scared shitless. You wouldn't know how or what to think about anything anymore.

But Cole saw our confusion coming, too. He had a remedy all prepared.

Meanwhile, Ryan and I ate the mousse ourselves.

CHAPTER 10

The night of Cole's visit, I was up ruminating until well after sunrise, at which point the pills and alcohol finally took hold, and then there was nothing I could do to stay awake. Luckily, I'd made plans to take the day off, and I had the twins looking after Companion. Cheryl was deep into a courtroom brawl up in Dallas, and I was going to watch her closing argument, then take her to my favorite local restaurant, a place that might have given Companion a run for its money if they weren't separated by a few hundred miles.

The Flexeril-gin combo had taken a toll, and at noon I was still slapping the snooze button every eight minutes. When I did finally manage to drag my ass out of bed, I had some trouble putting one foot in front of the other, and the pot of coffee and cool shower didn't get me to much more than a passable crawl. There's nothing more punishing than starting out a four-hour drive knowing that you don't have a hope in hell of arriving on time, and it only gets worse when you discover there's not much to distract you along the way—just a bottomless vista of dull brown earth that won't do a thing to lift your mood.

I kept the speedometer around ninety and forced myself to sing along to the eighties station, but still the minutes felt like hours, and I couldn't stop seeing Cole sitting there in my living room, telling me I now existed to serve him. *How are you going to get out of this one?* I asked myself, but the answer wasn't going to come that easy. No, this was a long-haul riddle, and the best I could hope for in the near term was to do no greater harm.

I managed to get to the courthouse before they'd wrapped up for the day, which means I got to spend some time watching Cheryl do her thing. I had to smile when I saw her. She was wearing a gray pantsuit and had her hair pulled back, but nothing short of a bag over her head could bring Cheryl down to the level of everyday folks. I asked once if she thought her beauty worked against her in court, but she just looked at me like I was too dumb to live.

She had a witness up on the stand when I took my seat. Turns out she was making so much hay cross-examining her client's little sister that she decided to go ahead and delay her closing. *Little* in this case refers to the sister's age: she must have weighed about four hundred pounds, and you could tell at a glance that her life to date hadn't been much fun. That didn't mean Cheryl would take it easy, though. As I alluded to before, Cheryl's an eye-on-the-prize kind of lawyer, and she'd drill down on the Dalai Lama's darkest moments if it was in her client's best interest.

She'd filled me in some on the case as the trial went along. Sarah, the sister on the stand, had a much rosier memory of her childhood home than did Cindy, the sister on trial, and that was a problem because Cindy had murdered her father for reasons Cheryl hoped to show were justifiable, or at least in the justifiable ballpark. In an effort to get her life on track, Cindy had drunk the AA Kool-Aid, which meant she'd been going around asking people to forgive her for all the wrong she'd done them. On May 1, 2010, she'd turned up at her dad's house with a box of chocolates and a handful of helium balloons that read "Sorry I Let You Down."

But her mea culpa fell on deaf ears. The father, it turns out, was two years into his battle with Alzheimer's and didn't know who his daughter was, let alone what she had to be sorry about. He was friendly, though. Friendlier than he'd ever been before, maybe because he believed she was someone else, someone named Maggie, and no amount of gentle correction would convince him otherwise.

The father's caretaker, a biracial gay man with a heavy Hispanic accent—a walking composite sketch of what had been her father's favorite prejudices—tied the balloons to a ficus tree and sat her at the dining room table where so many of her worst memories had been forged. According to Cindy, her father was a nonstop merry-go-round of abuse, a man who used to lock her and her sister in a closet under the stairwell while he burned their mother with cigarettes and told her to scream louder so the children could hear. Which was why Cindy had run off at sixteen, less than a year after her mother's suicide, and never looked back until now, when it would have been better for everyone if she'd stayed away.

Cindy and her father sat across the table from each other, the same table she'd eaten at nearly every night for the first sixteen years of her life. In fact, the house seemed oddly unchanged. Devin kept it much the way her mother had. Not a crumb or a speck of dust anywhere. The walls were the same shade of yellow. The cuckoo clock made the same hysterical screeching sound on the half hour. There was the same jagged scratch on the wood floor where, at age eleven, she'd cut into it with a kitchen knife just to see if anyone would notice.

What was missing were the people. Her mother, her sister, and, yes, her father, because this man sitting across from her had almost nothing in common with who he'd been thirty years ago. She didn't know what to say to him, or how to say it.

Of course, it didn't help that he was deaf, or at least it didn't help her: on his end, the conversation seemed to roll along just fine. In fact, he seemed much happier now than at any time during her childhood. He talked about the thumb-sized robot creatures who lived inside his couch and raided the refrigerator when he slept. He talked about his own nocturnal trips to Sweden, where he'd fish off a fjord and sing with the stars. He talked about the brass band that had moved in next door and would play any request he shouted over the fence. These things seemed to give him great pleasure, even joy. For someone so old and frail, he was animated, cheerful. His energy seemed to build as he spoke, while hers drained away, until she felt like she might just lay her head down on the table and go to sleep. She pinched her arm to keep her eyes from closing, then found herself wiping tears from her cheeks, though she had no sense that she'd been crying.

Clearly, she'd waited too long to play prodigal daughter. There was no conversation to be had, no father left to apologize to.

"Excuse me, I'll be right back," she said, then got up and left.

Without meaning to, she found herself at the local bar where her second boyfriend had paid for her first drink the day she turned fifteen. Like her parents' house, the place hadn't changed much. The small black-and-white television was now an HD wide-screen, and the sports banners had been updated, but there were still rips in the stools and a crack running through the mirror behind the bar.

She ordered an Alabama slammer, same as she had all those years ago. The bartender glanced at the wall clock as if to remind her that it was still early afternoon.

"I'm celebrating," she said, then didn't speak again for hours—just pointed whenever her glass needed filling.

A little after nightfall, she wound up back at her father's house. She hadn't been drunk in a year, and now she wondered why she'd ever deprived herself of something so magical. She felt high, but not sloppy. Everything seemed possible again. She'd send this Devin packing, take care of her father herself. It would be hard, but she'd see him through to the end. It was what she needed to do in order to heal. Sarah could have every penny of the inheritance, if there was any inheritance to be had.

But by the time she got back to the house, things had changed. Devin didn't want to let her in.

"I'm perfectly fine," she said, assuming he smelled the liquor on her.

"It's not you," he told her. "It's your father. He's . . ."

"What?"

"Lucid. Sometimes, for short periods, his memory comes back. He's his old self, except that he understands what is happening to him. That makes him . . ."

"Bitter?" she asked. "Mean? Spiteful? Violent?"

Devin nodded.

"Well, hallelujah," Cindy said. "That's the dad I remember."

She pushed her way inside, told Devin he could take the rest of the night off.

She found her father sitting in his armchair, watching a muted baseball game.

He looked up at her, then looked back at the TV.

"Can't hear a goddamn thing anyway," he said.

She sat across from him on the couch.

"You were here earlier," he said.

She nodded.

"I thought it would've been the fat one who came crawling back."

"Sarah takes care of you, Pop," Cindy said. "She's the one who sends Devin."

He ignored her, or didn't hear.

"Instead," he continued, "I get the slut. What is it you want? Come back to rob the place? I bet you took one look at me and thought I'd be your easiest payday yet. Am I right? Am I?"

He seemed more excited at the prospect of being right than angry at the thought of his own daughter stealing from him.

He continued talking. Cindy stopped listening. She'd heard it all before. Even after a thirty-year hiatus, he fell back into exactly the same monologue. She was a whore who neglected to get paid for her services. She probably couldn't help being a whore, since she was the spitting image of her mother. Her mother had fucked his best friend less than a year into their marriage. Did Cindy know that? She should, since that was her gene pool. Everybody should know what they'll spend their life ducking and dodging and generally failing to escape from.

"Better to spread your legs and let it happen," he said. "Nothing you can do about it anyway."

The alcohol started to change her, like she was just now absorbing it. And as she walked upstairs to retrieve the antique Luger from the shoebox where he'd kept it since before she was born, she couldn't decide who she'd be putting out of his misery: the dying man whose brain was set to sci-fi, or the miserable prick who'd spent his life doling out the kind of pain people don't recover from.

I'm sharing all of this to prove a point about Cheryl: once she takes up your cause, you've got a champion for life. She'll do things for you that you might never do for yourself. More than anything, she'll fight for you. And she doesn't care how knock-down, drag-out dirty the fight gets. She'll kill kittens or lie to Congress if that's what it takes.

According to Sarah, Cindy was the cause of all her family's problems. When her parents fought, it was over Cindy: Cindy's grades, the way Cindy dressed, the boys Cindy dated, the drugs they found in Cindy's room.

"Cindy was never going to get into college," Sarah said. "Not even a community college. My mother couldn't take that. She thought Cindy was some kind of genius who couldn't get out of her own way. She thought Cindy could be everything she never was, if she'd only get her act together. Raising Cindy was like giving up on her own dreams a second time."

"What about you?" Cheryl asked, pacing a few feet from the stand.

"What about me?"

"Didn't your mother have any hopes for you?"

The prosecutor objected, but the judge overruled. Sarah just shrugged.

"We'll come back to that," Cheryl said. "For now I'm interested in another question: you're sure your mother's suicide had nothing to do with your father torturing her?"

"How could it when that never happened?"

"So who was it that burned her flesh? Fractured her eye socket? Broke two of her ribs?"

"I told you, nobody. Those are Cindy's fantasies."

"Any idea how her fantasies turned up on your mother's autopsy?"

Cheryl scored a clear victory on that one: Sarah had no clue how to answer.

"It's my mother who was sick," she said. "In the head. Cindy too. She got my mother's illness."

"What illness is that?"

"The mental kind."

"You aren't aware of a specific diagnosis?"

"How could there be a diagnosis? Neither of them would go to a doctor. Neither of them would admit anything was wrong."

"And you? Would you admit anything was wrong?"

Cheryl had her back to me, but I could see her eyebrow rising as she cocked her head. I must have been the only person in that courtroom who understood just how much she was enjoying herself. That might sound like an indictment of her character—who enjoys emotionally dissecting one sister to prove that the other may have been at least a little bit justified in offing their demented father?— but that's not how I mean it. Maybe *enjoying* is the wrong word. What I'm trying to describe is more like a state of being. It's like you're hovering above the grit of your own life—the hangnails and insomnia and stomach pains, the petty distractions and impulses, the disappointments you've suffered and the ones you've caused— and you just keep rising up into a sphere where none of that exists. You aren't aware of anything anymore. You aren't outside of yourself, hemming and hawing, judging every little decision, thinking how it might be better to do this instead of that, use this word instead of that one. That's when you know you've succeeded: when you stop coming up with ways to measure your own success. But by then you aren't even asking the question anymore. And when you've been there yourself, when you know what it is to live outside of time and your own body, then watching someone else get there is a contact high. I'm not ashamed to say that it turned me on. Hungover and stressed as I was, I had a boner that would've made it awkward to stand just then.

"Oh, there was plenty wrong in my family," Sarah said. "I'm not disputing that. I'm just saying my father wasn't the source."

"So this isn't your revenge?"

"What isn't?"

"Your testimony here today."

"Revenge for what?"

"Your sister abandoned you, didn't she? You were only thirteen when she left you to fend for yourself."

"I was better off, believe me."

"Better off alone with your father?"

"That was the first time I knew any peace."

Cheryl walked back to the defendant's table, took up a folder, and flipped through the pages inside. Knowing Cheryl, she had whatever she was looking for memorized already and was just stalling to let the gravitas build up.

"You were hospitalized twice in the six months after your mother died," she said. "Can you tell us why?"

"That was thirty years ago."

"Are you saying you don't remember?"

"I'm saying you've got the paperwork right there. Why don't you tell me?"

"Because I want to hear *your* recollection. You say that you were happy living alone with your father. Looking at these reports, I wonder how that can be true."

"And I wonder how you could tell anything from a thirty-year-old piece of paper."

Here, I was expecting Cheryl to play the hostile-witness card, but she had a bigger endgame in mind. She did a little deliberate pacing, paused to stare down at her file some more, then picked back up.

"According to this first report, you fainted at a local park. Your friends called 911."

"We were on one of those playground spinners. We'd smoked some weed. I got dizzy."

Cheryl kept going like Sarah hadn't said a thing.

"Apparently you were five foot five and weighed sixty-eight pounds. The attending recommended that you be admitted and held until your weight rose to normal levels. Subsequent blood work revealed, and I'm quoting here, 'unequivocal signs of malnutrition.'"

"So? How many thirteen-year-old girls eat right?"

"True, but they did find other signs of abuse. Bruising on both arms. A patch of raw scalp where your hair had been ripped out."

"I was a tomboy. I liked to play rough."

"Yes, that's what you told the doctors. I guess you do remember."

The prosecutor objected.

"Withdrawn," Cheryl said. "All right, Sarah. Let's move on to the second hospital visit."

"Why? What's any of this got to do with my sister? She wasn't even there."

"Exactly. She wasn't there when you most needed her. When your mother had already abandoned you in the most violent and definitive way possible. When there was no one on hand to protect you from a father who—"

"I told you, I didn't need protecting."

Cheryl took another intense stare at the file in her hands.

"Let's look more closely at that second hospital visit," she said. "This time there was no 911 call: you just showed up at the ER. Does that sound right?"

"I don't remember."

"I doubt you would: you were barely conscious. Apparently you'd ingested a large amount of bleach. Doctors administered an endoscopy and kept you on an IV overnight. Any idea how or why you wound up drinking bleach during this otherwise peaceful time in your life?"

"It was an accident. Bleach and water look the same."

"And that's why toddlers often confuse the two. When you're, say, three years old, you'll grab something and swallow it on impulse, because it looks like something else you've ingested before. But by the time you're thirteen, you should recognize the odor. Not to mention the container. Unless you happened to have a water glass full of bleach lying around. And even then, the taste should have prevented you from drinking enough to do any damage."

"Like I said, I don't remember. I don't know how it happened."

"I see," Cheryl said.

She said the same two words to me on those rare occasions when we argued, and I knew damn well what they meant: she was about to let me have it.

"This is indelicate," she told Sarah, "but I want to focus on your weight for a moment. Your chart for this second visit lists you at one hundred thirty pounds. That's sixty pounds more than you weighed just two months prior. Is that a typo?"

"I was thirteen. It's called puberty."

"Sixty pounds in two months is extreme at any age."

"So first you say my father was starving me; then you say he was . . . what? Force-feeding me?"

"I don't believe I said either."

"So what are you saying?"

Her tone was more beleaguered than belligerent. You could tell that more than anything Sarah wanted a nap.

"I'm trying not to draw any conclusions, but there is one scenario that would make sense of the weight gain and loss, the bruises, the missing hair, the bleach."

Sarah did her best to seem nonplussed, but she couldn't keep herself from squirming and playing with her hair.

"It isn't uncommon for teenage girls—especially young teenage girls—to show up at an ER with a bellyful of bleach. Do you know why?"

Sarah's face was spinning through shades of red, and her eyes were welling up.

Cheryl stepped closer to the stand, made her voice as soft as she could without dropping the volume.

"Because they're pregnant, or think they might be," she said. "They don't want their parents to know. It's called a bleach abortion."

She reached out and touched Sarah's arm. I thought for sure Sarah would scream or pull away or lash out, but she didn't budge. Maybe she was glad for the human contact. More likely, she didn't notice.

"It was your father, wasn't it?" Cheryl said. "Once your sister left, there was nothing to stop him."

Sarah didn't confirm or deny, just collapsed with her head in her arms. The kind of collapse where you wonder if the person will ever get back up again. The prosecution turned apoplectic, and this time the judge sustained. It didn't matter, though. I looked over at the jury and saw right away that Cheryl had hit her mark. They understood now why Cindy had run off. They understood why the mother killed herself. Whether or not it was all-the-way true, they had their explanation. It was the father on trial now, and if they could have, I'm sure that jury would have let Cindy walk right then and there.

CHAPTER 11

etting a woman to admit her father was a rapist piece of shit might not seem like cause for celebration, but it was a big victory for Cheryl, and more importantly for Cindy, whose path to the minimum sentence just got a whole lot wider. You might think what Cheryl did to the poor sister—exposing her darkest and most damaging secret for all the world to gawk at—was about as low as it gets, but all Cheryl saw was the years that her client wouldn't spend in prison. For Cheryl, there was the greater good, period. I guess that bothered me a little at first, but now I'm inclined to agree with her. The older you get, the harder it is to believe in anything like a pure win.

Afterward, I took her to a place called Sale Pierre's. Pierre's was owned by a guy named Mike who'd never been to Paris or even New York, and there was nothing dirty about the place, though it was small and dark and tucked away in a neighborhood no tourist would ever find. Some nights they had a gypsy jazz duo playing in the back, but this wasn't one of them, and I was glad for it because I had things to talk about with Cheryl and needed a restaurant, not a listening room.

I ordered two glasses of champagne to start, and Cheryl asked the waiter to pour a little cassis in hers.

"We're celebrating, aren't we?" she said. "You told me you have news."

"I never said it was the kind you celebrate."

"I can celebrate anything if I put my mind to it."

She seemed a little tipsy already, with a kind of loose and coy smile, and a rogue strand of hair curling around one cheek. She took her blazer off and draped it over the back of her chair, and I was glad to see her in a sleeveless blouse.

"You were phenomenal today," I said.

"Relax," she said. "You're already getting some later."

"I'm serious," I told her. "You knew exactly where you needed to lead that woman, and I'm guessing she knew exactly where she didn't want to be led. It's one thing to make a path for yourself and then follow it; it's another thing to make a path for someone else and then trick them into following it against their own best interest."

"That's where you're wrong," Cheryl said. "Sarah wanted all of that to come out. She was desperate for it to come out. She has been for a very long time."

"You talk to her in advance or something? Work it out between you?"

"Of course. Same with the judge and jury. I'd never take a case otherwise."

There was a confused beat where I showed how gullible I could be, then a longer beat where Cheryl laughed at me a little harder than she needed to.

"Everybody wants to talk about how they were broken," she said. "Everybody thinks their personal story will somehow solve the riddle that is the human condition. They just need a little push to get past the shame."

"I guess," I said, though right then I was in no particular hurry to unburden myself.

The waiter, a French kid likely here on a student visa, set down our drinks and took our order. I asked for an endive salad and the coq au vin; Cheryl, who'd learned to trust me in culinary matters, ordered the same. As far as I'm concerned, coq au vin is the absolute best way to eat your wine, and whoever worked behind the curtain at

Sale Pierre's used a top-notch burgundy. The diced portobellos were a nice touch, too.

"Are you offended?" Cheryl asked.

"Offended?"

"Garçon didn't recognize you. The chef hasn't come running out to shake your hand."

That had happened once or twice before, and it wasn't unusual for a stranger to interrupt our meal by demanding my autograph. One well-meaning older woman actually said, "You're that guy who cooks for the dead, aren't you?" "The almost-dead," Cheryl had corrected.

But it was hard to imagine anyone making a fuss over me at Sale Pierre's. It just wasn't that kind of place. It was too far off the beaten path, too far outside the mainstream. At six o'clock on a weeknight, we had the main room to ourselves, and I doubt *Last Supper* was on a twentysomething French national's radar. If it had been, I'm sure he wouldn't have approved. I didn't really approve myself, which is why I downed my champagne in one quick shot and started looking for the waiter to bring our first bottle of wine.

"Thirsty?" Cheryl asked.

I nodded like I was responding to some other, more soul-probing question.

"All right," she said. "Lay it on me."

I laid some of it on her—the smallest part possible. I told her a big-time producer wanted to take *Last Supper* national. I didn't say anything about Cole, and of course I didn't mention Louis: Cheryl was very fond of Louis. I figured I'd play dumb for as long as I could, then ease into my story about the old man riding off into the Argentine sunset. Cheryl would like that: she was big on people chasing their dreams, especially in their waning years. She'd probably want to go visit him—she was always after me about traveling—but I'd cross that bridge when we got to it. Right now, I was more worried about the Cole bridge. He'd threatened to put in regular appearances at Companion, and I was already having waking nightmares about what might happen if he and Cheryl came face-to-face.

Cheryl started to raise her glass for a toast, then looked at me and set it back down again.

"I don't get it," she said. "Isn't this good news?"

I should have said it was. I should have sold it as the best damn news to ever come my way. I mean, I had no choice in the matter, at least for now, so why not pretend it had been my idea from the jump, the thing I'd always wanted, the thing that would help me put my stamp on this world. But my heart wasn't in it, so I just kind of shrugged and nodded.

"Are you sure?" she asked. "Because you look like someone just told you your dog has cancer."

"I don't have a dog."

"I'm aware. Seriously, James, this is fantastic. You'll have a national platform."

I'd prepared myself for everything but her enthusiasm.

"It's kind of an ugly way to make a name for yourself," I said.

"Oh, I didn't mean it was fantastic for you. Maybe it would be if you were doing it pro bono and off the record, just driving around and cooking final meals out of the goodness of your heart, though even then I'd say your charitable impulses were probably misdirected. I mean, who has the stomach to eat well when they know they'll be dead in an hour? But let's be honest: *Last Supper* is just garish rubbernecking. Pro-murder propaganda. Mankind couldn't reach much lower if it tried."

I hoped the candlelight was too dim for her to see me squirming. Sometimes when Cheryl's had a good day in court, the aggression carries over.

"So who the hell is it good for?" I asked.

"Ryan," she said. "Who else?"

"How?"

She looked at me like I was a pitched battle between mental deficiency and moral bankruptcy.

"No one wants to kill a celebrity," she said. "Not even a celebrity by association. The death penalty is barbaric, but it continues because we only kill the poor and marginalized. It's easy to ignore because the people it affects—I mean the families, not just the inmates—have no public voice. But shine a spotlight on the electric chair, metaphorically speaking, and you might start to see protesters from around the globe gathered outside the Capitol building. Texas likes killing people. The state won't jeopardize the law that lets them do it."

"So a national show will pressure the DA to reduce Ryan's sentence?"

She nodded.

"You haven't signed a contract yet, have you?"

"No."

"Good," she said. "We'll have to make sure there's no gag order. I'll need you in front of a camera every chance you get, talking about what a sweet kid Ryan was, how young he was when your parents died, what a miserable human being your aunt was. Where was the state then? What did they do to keep Ryan off the streets, make sure he grew into an upstanding citizen? It's only after the fact that they want to protect society. They show up at the end to execute someone they never cared about saving in the first place. Last year, the state of Texas killed thirteen people. The country killed fifty-two. That makes the USA a serial killer. That's the story you have to tell."

I could see her wheels spinning now. She was thinking past Ryan to her larger crusade, which was fine by me if it kept her energized. Not that Cheryl ever lacked energy. And I'll admit she had me feeling a little better. If I was going to sell my soul on the nation's largest stage, I at least ought to get a lifetime with my brother in return.

The waiter brought our coq au vins. I sat back and let Cheryl take the first bite. She shut her eyes and pushed out a little moan. I was glad not to have led her astray, but I wasn't beyond feeling a little jealous, too. My mind raced back, searching out her reaction to the last meal I'd cooked for her: the sea bass Cole had finished off. All I could remember was her pushing away the water chestnuts with the edge of her fork. She took another bite of her chicken and locked eyes with me. For a moment I thought she'd read my mind and was about to tell me that, good as her meal was, I had no rival in the kitchen.

But Cheryl was never the kid-gloves type.

"Just don't blow it," she said. "If you come off unsympathetic, it could actually hurt Ryan."

"I'll do my best," I said. "What about your corrupt-cop-protected-by-the-mayor angle?"

"Still working on it," she said. "The more angles we have, the better."

CHAPTER 12

Cole didn't waste any time: he had his hotshot producer at Companion before the week was out. I had to turn away paying customers at prime dinnertime just so we could all sit by the window—three of us at a table for six. It's unlikely I'd have taken a shine to this producer under any circumstances, but I flat-out couldn't stand the son of a bitch. To begin with, his name was Timothy, and he insisted you pronounce all three syllables. If you slipped up and called him Tim, he'd jump on you like a schoolmarm slapping the slow kid's hand. Second, he'd dumped a full canister of gel in his hair when what he really needed was dandruff shampoo. Like I said before, I'm not queasy by nature. I've cooked brain and tongue and testicles and about a hundred different kinds of insect, but there's something unseemly about large flakes of scalp stuck to a glistening head of jet-black hair. You start to see those flakes floating in your drink. You feel them crunching when you bite into your food, like large bits of tasteless salt.

But that's just me being petty. There were real reasons to dislike Timmy beyond the mere fact of his association with Cole. He was all bluster, talking in fits about his unbridled success, and always in terms of ratings and dollars. You could tell straight off that quality was the last thing he cared about. He may not have been breaking bones in back alleys, but he was pure gangster when it came to the bottom line, and in case you're wondering, he was all in on the drug smuggling. And not just the smuggling. Timmy got up to go to the bathroom more than once, and each time he came back his nostrils looked a little worse for wear.

He didn't comment one way or the other on his duck fajitas, and he went on about himself for so long that I started to wonder why he'd wanted to meet me at all. But then he made his reason crystal clear. He leaned out over the table with his elbows straddling his plate and said, "What if you get caught?"

"Doing what?" I asked.

In hindsight, I understand just how stupid that must have sounded, but Timmy had been droning on, and I was startled when he interrupted himself to ask me a question.

"What do you think?" he asked. His tone made me wonder how many personal assistants he'd shitcanned over the years.

"He won't get caught," Cole said. "They don't search his car on the way in. That's why this will work."

Timmy didn't take his eyes off me. "But what if he does?"

I knew what he was asking then.

"It's my operation," I said. "You had no idea."

"You might want to rehearse that a bit. It didn't sound very convincing."

"Don't worry," Cole said. "If the time ever comes, he'll be more than convincing. I've given him every incentive. He confesses to this crime, and other, more serious crimes come to light."

"Such as?"

"It's better if you don't know. At least for now."

Timmy started to protest but remembered who he was talking to in time to stop himself. We discussed the smuggling logistics in a restaurant whisper, and then they left, sticking me with a three-hundred-dollar tab. I tipped our waiter a full 30 percent because Timmy hadn't treated him any better than he'd treated me.

•

We started the operation two weeks later with a trial run to Hunts-ville. Per Cole's instructions, I got up at four in the morning and dropped the BMW at a shop called AutoBody. You could see on the sign that it used to be somebody's AutoBody, but the current owner had scraped away the old name without bothering to replace it. I pulled up outside, honked three times, left the key in the igni-tion, and walked away. I'd suggested to Cole that we might find a mechanic closer to Huntsville, if only to avoid driving two hundred miles in a car full of H, but he wouldn't hear it. He said he knew and trusted this guy, which meant he had something to hold over him.

I had an hour to kill at a time of day when almost nothing was open, in a neighborhood where there wasn't much to see or do anyway. The shop was just under a mile from Cole's old rec center, a place I hadn't laid eyes on for fifteen years. Back when Ryan and I more or less lived there, it felt like we were making good memories, ones we'd enjoy reliving well into our twilight years. All that was soured and undone now, but I was still curious as to what became of the place after Cole went away, and I had nowhere else to be.

A short walk later, I found myself standing in the dark out-side a training facility for the Austin PD. The city had turned the building into a baby-cop factory, and the irony made me smile for what I guessed would be the last time all day. I stood across the street watching recruits pour in at a little after five in the morning, looking like their mommies had just dragged them out of bed by the hair. The city must have seized Cole's property when they busted him, a thought that made me shiver, wondering what they'd do with Companion when the time came, because in the back of my mind I already had a dark notion about how this all would end, how any-thing that involved Cole would have to end.

But meanwhile there was good news: an entrepreneurial vendor had set up his cart at the academy entrance and was plying the cadets with caffeine and sugar. You might think I'd be a snob about any-thing edible, but every culinary experience comes with a context, and sometimes a jelly donut is as good as eggs Florentine, and sometimes Styrofoam-infused coffee is just the thing to start your gears turning. So I moved to the end of a longish line and wondered if any of these kids ahead of me might one day slap the cuffs on. And then my mind just kind of drifted.

I'm sure the early hour had something to do with it, but I started to hatch a fantasy, or maybe I should call it a contingency plan. I listened for what people were buying and scanned the prices on the board. The baby cops were dropping close to five bucks apiece, and now there were more of them lined up behind me than ahead of me. In a peak hour, the vendor probably pulled in three hundred dollars, maybe more. He was alone in his truck, which meant the truck itself was most of his overhead. If times got tough, he could cross rent right off his expense list: all he'd have to do was park at a Walmart, grab some sleep, then shower at the Y. It'd be the perfect cover for a fugitive. Nobody notices the food truck guy. He's just some greaser listening to AM radio while he doles out his wares. No one knows his name, and most days his longest conversation lasts a few minutes. So when things turned hot with Cole . . .

Waiting in line, I started to see myself manning a food truck in some exotic, non-extradition city—Buenos Aires, maybe—selling coffee and crepes and anything else I could make quickly in a small space. I delved into the details, drafting menus and prices and coming up with fake names for myself. I'd let my hair grow long, keep a constant five-o'clock shadow. I'd disguise my voice with a lisp or a tic. And on the off chance anyone ever asked, I'd make up a personal history they'd have one hell of a time disproving. Maybe I grew up in a holler in Appalachia. Maybe my parents were backwoods hippies who raised me on an Alaskan commune. Good luck at the Hall of Records.

It was sounding like a great adventure, and for a minute I found myself wishing my life would blow up so I could strike out on the lam. But like most fantasies, it didn't account for losing what I already had. Or *who* I had, because no way would I ever see Ryan or Cheryl again. Still, there was some comfort in dreaming up another life, and I guess that was the point. Everyone wants to believe there are other possibilities just lining up behind whatever it is they're doing now.

I kept up my plotting as I walked around the old neighborhood, eating a donut and drinking twenty-two ounces of singed caffeine.

These were the streets Ryan and I used to walk, and for the most part they hadn't changed. The houses were the same little boxes, some well maintained and some in disrepair, some with immaculate lawns and flower boxes in the windows, others fronted by heaps of junkyard trash. It all looked poorer than I remembered, and it struck me, in a way it never had when I was a kid, that there are two kinds of working poor: there's the kind who have given up imagining any other life, and the kind who are maintaining their good habits so they'll be ready when it's time to graduate. And maybe there's a third kind: the kind who are fine right where they are. People who get through the day on life's small pleasures. Planting their flowers, reading a book, taking a walk early in the morning when they have the world to themselves. They're the ones who'll inherit the earth, and I hope I'm around to see it.

•

By the time I got back to the auto shop, the BMW was sitting in the lot out front, gleaming like it had been buffed and polished. The mechanic, whose face I'd never see, had left an invoice for an oil change on the passenger seat, which was one more little piece of what Cole had called my "plausible deniability." As soon as I could, I planned to stop and give the car a thorough search; see if I could figure out where they'd put the shipment, or if there really was a shipment. Maybe this first run was a test. Maybe they wanted to see if I'd go sprinting to the cops.

But Cole's paranoia ran deeper than that. He must have suspected I'd take off with his supply, because the square-jawed thug in the vanilla sedan wasn't subtle about tailing me. I drove the same square block twice, and he was still there, a few feet from my bumper. I pulled into a 7-Eleven for an iced coffee, and when I came back out, he was there. No doubt about it: I had an escort. It made me wonder how many guys Cole had on his payroll. First there was Ryan's CO, who might or might not be the same guy who would unpack the car at Huntsville; then there was the mechanic, who might or might not be the same guy tailing me. But then there'd have to be a mechanic and a CO in Oklahoma and Florida and at every stop on my death row tour. Cole hadn't been out more than a few months. He must have started planning while he was inside, not long after *Last Supper* started to air. Did they watch the show in gen pop? Or did he have someone keeping tabs on me all along?

The thing I really couldn't understand was why I felt wounded, like Cole not trusting me hurt my feelings. Like he was still the father figure and I was still aching for his approval. I guess there's a part of our childhood that we never leave behind, no matter what's come to pass in the meantime.

Get over it, I told myself. *Cole conned you when you were a kid, but you're not a kid anymore. You'll find your way out of this. Just keep stalling.*

So I took a deep breath, pulled onto the highway, waved to my babysitter, and played by the rules. No unnecessary stops, cruise control set to sixty miles per hour. But my nerves wouldn't quit, and the closer we got to Huntsville, the higher I had to crank the AC, because I sweat waterfalls when I'm agitated. Cole knew this about me, and I wondered if that was why he'd left Louis in the freezer—if that had been his idea of an inside joke.

•

Instead of the usual dread, I felt some relief when I saw the film crew at the gates. Familiar faces can be a kind of safe zone, even if you don't much like the people they're attached to. And I was damn glad to be rid of my escort. He'd stuck to me for all those miles like the heavy breathing in a horror film. From here it would be business as usual, provided Cole's inside man didn't botch the job. On top of which I'd convinced myself that my deniability really was plausible. Creaky, but plausible, because I never did see the product, and I didn't know for sure that there was a shipment to be off-loaded. I thought a good lawyer should be able to work with that.

Maybe the strangest part of the day was that this turned out to be our best episode yet. For once, I had an honest-to-God connection with the inmate. We went to the same high school, albeit a decade apart, and we'd both been flunked twice by the same algebra teacher. Ron, the inmate, was a sweet little guy with owl-rimmed glasses, and I actually did feel sorry for him, because it sounded to me like his pastor had it coming. The fact that the pastor's grown daughter walked in at exactly the wrong moment was just one of life's unhappy accidents.

And Ron had good taste in food, too. He asked for one of my favorite dishes, or at least one of my favorite dishes to cook: spaghetti squash with turkey meatballs. There's something therapeutic about scraping squash flesh with the tines of a fork, and there's very little you can't do with a lump of uncooked turkey.

It wasn't until later, when I was cooking for Ryan, that something in me broke. I was alone in the conjugal apartment, prepping a spinach lasagna and deciding what I would and wouldn't tell Ryan about my new working relationship with Cole. I had the spinach and ricotta and Romano and oregano and garlic and basil all spread out on the counter and ready to go. But then as I started mixing them together in one big bowl, I lost sight of what I was doing and why. I couldn't separate the smell of the garlic from the smell of the oregano. I couldn't remember or imagine what basil tasted like. And the sight of all those ingredients blending together just confused me. It was like I was speaking words I couldn't understand. They sounded right, but I had no idea what they meant. No idea why I'd picked those words and not other words. No faith that someone else would understand me, either. There was no joy in it. I had this sudden feeling that I'd rather be anywhere else, doing anything else. And somehow I knew that feeling wasn't going away.

CHAPTER 13

That first delivery must have gone off without a hitch, because I didn't hear anything from anyone. Not from the cops. Not from Cole or Timmy. Life just returned to normal, in a Stepford kind of way. I went around impersonating myself, or what I thought I knew of myself. It was like I'd studied my own behavior from a distance: I could mimic my movements, but I had no idea what they meant. Like I had nothing in common with myself anymore. I wanted to blame Cole, but I knew it couldn't be all his fault.

I told Ryan that Cole had been in contact, but I didn't tell him much more. I figured he had enough on his mind. He didn't need to know *why* the new CO had decided to lay off, any more than he needed to know why *Last Supper* was going national.

I didn't tell Cheryl about Cole, either. I wanted to, but there was just no upside to it. When everything came out—and I had no doubt it would—she'd be crazy to stay with me. Our relationship had a sell-by date, but only I knew it. Why not keep making memories while we could?

She asked about Louis. I said it wasn't unusual for him to disappear for long stretches, but I promised to check on him. I wasn't ready to trot out the Argentina lie just yet. It made me a little sad thinking that she was the first and only person to ask after my former partner. I knew Louis was retired, and I knew his family had dwindled to nothing, but I hadn't spent much time considering how isolated he was. Cole, on the other hand, had picked up on it right away.

•

A month went by before Timmy was ready to start shooting. He would have needed longer, but like Cole, he'd started prepping before I was on board. No one told me anything about the inmate in advance. My new director, a guy named William Storey, believed in capturing spontaneous reactions. He'd gone to UCLA and had a short-lived brush with fame when he made a feature-length B movie called *Flesh Stalkers*. "Flesh stalkers" were zombies who still had their intellectual and emotional faculties. I made it through the first hour on YouTube before I gave up. The main character was a professor of Shakespeare turned stalker, and the highlight came for me when he quoted Hamlet: he could count himself king of infinite space, if only his skin wasn't sloughing off.

The film didn't improve much past the premise. The fake blood looked like strawberry preserves (I froze a frame, and I swore I saw seeds), and I recognized the main actor from a car-insurance commercial where he shared triple billing with a parakeet and a boa constrictor. I googled the poor bastard and found he went to Juilliard. There are so many ways to fail in life, sometimes I think it's a miracle anyone pans out.

Like I said, they didn't tell me anything about the inmate I'd be cooking for or the facility I'd be cooking in: they just gave me an itinerary and warned me against missing my flight. I'm embarrassed to say it, but I'd never been out of state. I never had the money to travel before I opened Companion, and once I had the money I didn't have the time. Oklahoma wouldn't have been my first choice, but as far as flying goes, it wasn't a bad way to get my feet wet: it's a short trip, and you don't hit much turbulence when you're cruising over the flattest part of the world. And Timmy's production company sprang for first class, which was probably wasted on me, since I'd never flown coach, though the complimentary beverages did slow my nerves.

We landed in Tulsa at nine in the evening. Timmy and his team arranged to have a car that looked almost exactly like mine waiting at the airport. From there, a preprogrammed GPS led me right to a luxury hotel in the heart of downtown, a fourteen-story flatiron affair with a marble fountain in the lobby and two glass elevators. My room wasn't palatial, but the shower had two showerheads, the tub was jetted, and the flat-screen TV covered most of one wall. I set my suitcase down on the spare bed and scanned the channels. There were about a hundred porn flicks to choose from, and while part of me would have welcomed the distraction, another part of me knew I'd feel like shit afterward.

I needed to do something, though. I was having the kind of half-horny, half-suicidal crisis that comes with being alone in a strange city, the kind of crisis that makes you feel like your loins might explode. The kid at the front desk had been hard-selling the hotel's roof bar, which was open until midnight and had won a bunch of regional awards, and I figured it was in my own professional interest to check it out. I wasn't looking for anything more than a little conversation, but that didn't stop me from imagining a long train of attractive businesswomen lining the zinc. I changed into my tightest jeans and splashed a little cologne on my neck. Of course, when I got up there all I found was a middle-aged barkeep in a bow tie and a piano player on break because he had no customers to play for. Maybe this was a luxury hotel, but it was still a weeknight in Tulsa; and while the view of the skyline might have been every bit as spectacular as the desk clerk had led me to believe, it was still the Tulsa skyline.

The pianist asked if I had any requests, but I told him not to bother: I was tone-deaf and wouldn't be staying long anyway. I ordered a kir and carried it to a two-top beside an ivory-covered brass railing that wouldn't have stopped the least-determined jumper. It was a beautiful night—cool for that time of year, without a speck of humidity. My drink was far sweeter than it should have been, but I didn't have the heart or energy to ask for another; I just sipped and stared down at the empty street, watching the traffic lights cycle through their colors. The piano started up behind me, a jazz ballad I didn't recognize or have any particular interest in. I'm sure this sounds ignorant, but I've never understood the point of a ballad: don't most people feel tired and melancholy as it is?

I kept watching the street, waiting for a single pedestrian to show himself, but none ever did. My mind wouldn't stray too far from any fantasy that had Cole back in prison and me still free. I kept thinking up ways he might violate his parole—ways that couldn't be traced back to me. I thought about lacing one of his dinners with cannabis. I thought about plying him with liquor at Companion and making an anonymous phone call when he climbed in his car. I thought of ways to get him on camera socializing with another felon. But I'd be the first one he'd suspect in every case, and besides, I knew damn well his parole officer had to be on the payroll. There was a universe of calculation behind every risk Cole took, and for all my thinking, I kept circling back to slightly altered versions of the same plan: *Keep him happy while I bide my time.*

I finished my drink, topped it off with a quick calvados, and told the bartender he could charge it to my room. Back downstairs, I swallowed two Ambien and got into bed.

The pills-and-liquor routine would probably kill me sooner than later, but everyone's got to die of something, and this wasn't the time to be quitting bad habits.

•

You get a sense of freedom waking up alone in a city where no one knows you, even when you aren't in that city of your own volition, even when what you are is the very opposite of free.

At five o'clock I rolled onto my side, picked up the phone, and ordered the most expensive breakfast room service had to offer. Then I took a double-headed shower and dried myself under a heat lamp while I waited on delivery. The smoked salmon was rubbery and required more chewing than I would have liked, but the four-cup pot of French roast had just the right kick.

From Tulsa, the GPS led me to a sprawling salvage yard outside
a town called Beggs. The sun was just coming up when I got there,
and I can't say daylight improved the place any. I pulled in front of
a shed that looked like it was built to house power tools, though the
flower box and American flag suggested people lived there. What I
guess you'd call the lawn was littered with car parts—everything
from fenders to the light bar off a police cruiser. I got out and started
toward the door, but a man's voice yelling through a curtained
window stopped me.

"You see that trailer on the other side of the clearing?"

I turned and looked—first for anything that might be called a
clearing, then for the trailer. I spotted it maybe fifty yards away, separated from where I was standing by a minefield of rusted and rotting
junk. It was white, or had been once, with buckling linoleum siding
and an antenna up top that looked like an abstract sculpture made of
soda cans and outsize coat hangers.

"Yeah, I see it," I said.

"Well, you can head on in there and take a nap if you like. The
couch is real comfy. When you hear me honk long-short, long-short,
you count to thirty, then come back out. You'll be good to go."

"All right," I said.

Like with the other mechanic, I wasn't supposed to see his face,
though this time it seemed kind of pointless, since he lived on the
premises and I'd have no trouble finding the place again. But I guess
by not seeing him load up the car I was adding to my plausible
deniability—and his, too.

Inside, the trailer was about what you'd expect. Plastic paneling
and a synthetic beige carpet they'd given up cleaning years ago. There
was a swimsuit calendar hanging crooked on the wall when you first
walked in, open to a picture of a blonde model with her hair teased
about a foot off her head. When I looked a little closer, I saw she was
representing January 1987, and I figured that was probably around
the time they bought this trailer, because nothing in it looked less
than twenty years old. Even the junk—the head off a cigar-store
Indian, an ornate banjo with no strings, a gramophone with a crack

running through the horn—had an antique quality about it, like this was the good stuff they wanted to keep out of the rain.

The couch he'd mentioned was a six-foot-long knockoff Chesterfield patched here and there with duct tape, but it really was comfortable, even if I didn't dare rest my head on that grease-stained pillow. I lay there as instructed and shut my eyes, then opened them again and looked around some more. The windows were boarded up with plywood, but the cracks let in enough light to see by.

My imagination started churning. It wasn't the kind of space you'd ever expect to be in, and I'm a daydreamer by nature. Most chefs are, I guess, since so much of what we do is by rote. More and more, my dreams focused on hiding, and this place seemed built for someone who didn't want to be found. Whether it was Buenos Aires or Beggs, I guess there'd come to be a feeling of inevitability about my flight.

So I played a little game with myself. I looked around the trailer and thought: What if this was it? What if this one long room was all I had for the rest of my life, and I could never leave? Step outside and go to jail or be shot: that was the rule. What would I do with myself from now to the end of days? Assuming, I thought, that an intelligent person is never bored. And assuming I was intelligent, which may have been a reach. Ryan and I never had much of an education. K through twelve (or eleven for Ryan: he dropped out on his sixteenth birthday) was mostly about waiting for the final bell. We'd picked up a thing or two at the rec center, but none of that was book learning.

I'd always been interested in history—in all the names I recognized but knew nothing about. Napoléon and Genghis Khan and Joan of Arc and Malcolm X and Amelia Earhart and Ralph Waldo Emerson, who my high school was named after. So my first thought was that I'd go on a reading jag, provided I could find some kind of local liaison to bring me books. If not, maybe I'd find a way to string up that banjo and teach myself to play. Or I'd finally make a practice out of all those yoga poses Cheryl had taught me.

The point is, even locked away in a trailer, there were possibilities. Whenever I considered those possibilities, I found myself getting excited in an over-caffeinated, can't-slow-my-heartbeat kind of way. And more and more, I was starting to question things I'd never questioned before. Why did I live where I lived? Why did I do what I did? It all seemed random, like I'd arrived at the scene of an accident and never left.

But one thing was sure: I'd never know any other life until I got out from under Cole.

CHAPTER 14

I left the salvage yard expecting to find an Oklahoma chaperone in my rearview mirror, but I was all by my lonesome. I thought about pulling over and taking the car apart just to scratch an itch, but I've never been handy with vehicles, and there was a good chance I wouldn't be able to get it back together again. Besides which, it was thundering and raining so hard I couldn't see too far beyond the windshield. I thought about the rain while I drove. I wondered what it would be like to wake up on the day you were set to die and see a biblical mess pouring down. Would you think that storm was somehow made for you? That God was showing his disapproval or his sympathy? Or maybe just giving you a dramatic send-off? That is, if you happened to believe in God. And if you happened to have a window in your cell.

The penitentiary I was headed for sat outside a town called McAlester. By the time I got to the city limits, the rain had let up and there was even a little post-storm sun drying things off. To say that McAlester isn't the most modern place would be a *Guinness Book* understatement. Even as you're driving down Main Street in a state-of-the-art luxury vehicle, you're surprised to look out and see other cars. Like you should be surrounded by shitkickers on horseback with dust swirling up everywhere and a nervous-looking sheriff pacing in front of the jail. Which makes sense, I guess, since the major industry in Mc-Alester is killing people. Besides the prison with its death row wing, there's a munitions plant that manufactures most of the bombs used by all branches of the US military.

The GPS led me right to the prison's main gate, where a camera crew three times the size of the Austin amateur hour was set up and waiting. A guy holding a neon-orange semaphore with a *Last Supper* insignia stitched down the side waved me over about fifty yards shy of the entrance, and then a golf cart drove up and a quartet of techies jumped out and started rigging the BMW with interior and exterior cameras.

I didn't like that one bit.

In the local-cable version you could barely tell it was me driving, except for one little tick where I rolled down my window and flashed an ID at the guards. Now they wanted up-close reaction shots, but there wasn't anything for me to react to. I mean, a prison's a prison. Some look ancient and haunted and some look like a community college campus, but either way you know what you're in for once you've spotted the barbed wire. I said as much to the guy with the semaphore, who seemed to be in charge of this advance party.

"Am I supposed to do anything?" I asked. "Look a certain way? Sing along to the radio?"

"Nah, just react, man," he said. "Bill likes to keep things simple."

I didn't tell him things already seemed pretty complicated to me. And they only got worse once I drove through the gates. Bill was waiting there, standing with his arms akimbo, flashing a smile that was meant to be welcoming but looked more like, *Time is money, and it's already wasting.*

When Bill and I talked on the phone, I'd pictured him tall, with an athletic build, but he was typically pear-shaped for a middle-aged guy, with curly salt-and-pepper hair and a decades-old denim jacket that he refused to take off even in eighty-degree weather. We exchanged the usual pleasantries, and then he asked me to drive back out and come in again.

"Did I do something wrong?" I asked.

"No, no, not at all," he said. "I just want to have alternatives to choose from later on."

Well, he wound up with a half dozen choices, which was putting too fine a point on it for my liking. Even the COs in the gatehouse were rolling their eyes. From there, I was directed to a visitor's parking spot, and Bill and I had a little powwow while we waited for the CO who'd escort us to the inmate's cell. I asked for a briefing on the guy I was about to interview, and Bill's eyes got real big.

"You mean you don't know anything about him?" he asked.

"How would I? No one's told me anything."

"It's an execution," Bill said. "It's been in the news. I just assumed you'd . . . But this is excellent. This is much better."

"What is?" I asked.

"Your coming to him with no preconceptions, no prejudices."

"Well, I imagine he did something very bad."

"The same way your brother did something bad. But there's more to your brother than that thing he did. There's a history. There's everything that led him to that moment."

"I just need to know what the guy likes to eat," I said.

"Wrong."

"Wrong?"

"The wrong approach entirely. Food is just a lens into a life that's ending, if you'll excuse the cinematic metaphor."

I said I would excuse it, but deep down that was a lie. You could tell Bill believed in his own intellect, and he had no qualms about being profound at someone else's expense. Whoever this inmate was, whatever he'd done, he deserved better than to spend his last minutes as a case study.

"The food is just a bonding mechanism," Bill went on. "A way to get him talking, get him to open up. Because what he has to share is exceedingly precious. Nobody knows for sure if they'll live through the day, but only a rare few know they won't. That's the essence of this show. That's what I want you to mine in your interview. The food itself is secondary."

The poor sap didn't realize he'd dropped a hundred grand on film school so that he could serve as front man for a drug dealer. He thought he was making a real documentary. Something for the time capsule.

"So you want me to go up there ice-cold and just start talking?"

"Is that a problem?"

"I liked it better the other way," I said.

"I've seen the results of the other way. Let's try mine."

Bill and I were getting off on the wrong foot, but I can't say I cared much. He was expendable, and I wasn't. And if acting like a prima donna made Cole's life just a little bit more difficult, well, that was a bonus.

"How about this?" I said. "How about you brief me on this asshole or I walk?"

I guess I'd raised my voice without meaning to, because suddenly people were watching. Bill scratched at his head and looked around for help like I'd backed him into a corner, which I have to admit felt pretty good because I was operating out of a pretty tight corner myself. Maybe that's how the world works, with each of us backing someone else into a corner, like we're all just chess pieces lining up one behind the other.

As if to prove my theory, a car door slammed a couple of spaces away, and there came Timmy, scraggly and unsmiling.

"Timothy," Bill said, giving a kiss-ass little bow.

"Is there a problem?" Timmy asked.

"Just an artistic difference," Bill said. "James wants me to prep him for his interview. I think it would be better if he knew no more about the inmate than the inmate knew about him."

"I see," Timmy said.

He turned so that we were standing almost toe to toe, his wide frame blocking Bill out altogether.

"I think that's our guard making his way over here, so let's set this straight real quick," he said. "The director directs. That's what he's here for. You take his directions. I don't care if he wants you in ballet slippers and a gas mask. You don't ask why. That's how we do things."

I'd be lying if I said my brain didn't go straight to picturing both their heads popping under the wheels of a garbage truck. I threw in the crew, too. The camera people and the gaffers and gophers and the makeup artist and the guy with the semaphore. Anyone who happened to be standing around. Go ahead and call me immature, but only if you've never had similar fantasies.

CHAPTER 15

They had the cameras and lighting in place before they let me enter the cell. The inmate sat on his bed, giggling to himself, embarrassed but also a little thrilled to have so many guests at one time. At first glance he was all facial hair—gleaming bald up top but with a red-and-white beard that straggled down to his gut. Despite Bill's efforts to create suspense, or maybe because of them, nothing about the guy shocked me, though I was taken aback by the cat on his lap: a brindled tabby with mazelike markings and a string collar around its neck.

You could see right away that the cat was the center of this guy's world, and vice versa. They kind of nuzzled and patted each other, the inmate deep-massaging the animal's neck while the cat head-butted his stomach over and over. I sat across from them on my stool and made a mental note to ask why the tabby was on death row.

But first I needed to know the inmate's name. Bill hadn't even told me that much. I thought it would seem unprofessional to ask, so I said, "Why don't you tell the people watching your name?"

He looked around at the crew crammed into his tiny cell, and I knew he thought I meant them: they were the ones watching. He didn't understand what the cameras were for any more than his cat did.

"I'm Wyatt," he said.

"And what about your friend?" I asked, nodding at the tabby.

"Cat Two," he said.

"Cat Two?"

"They gave me another one, but she died."

"I'm sorry to hear that," I said.

"It's okay. I like this one better. She keeps me calm."

"Is that why they gave her to you?"

Wyatt shrugged.

"We all got one," he said. "Everybody who wanted one. The cats used to live outside, but they got lonely."

"What about you?" I asked. "Were you lonely?"

He shrugged again, and I could tell *lonely* was a word someone had fed him; the concept was more than he could juggle.

"Let's talk about you," I said. "Why are you here?"

"You mean in prison?"

I nodded. He looked down, traced a line on Cat Two's coat with his pinky finger.

"I hurt my aunt," he said. "I'm sorry."

"How did you hurt her?"

"In the neck."

"Why did you hurt her?"

"She made me mad."

"How?"

"I cut her. I'm sorry."

He made a stabbing motion with his hand.

"I mean, how did she make you mad?"

He grunted, and his grip on the cat must have tightened, because she started squirming up a storm.

"I told her it wasn't me," he said.

"What wasn't you?"

Words were failing him now. His face turned a shade darker than his freckles, and his right leg started keeping frantic time. There was only right now for Wyatt. He couldn't remember an event without reliving it, without being there as if the years between had never happened.

It took him a while, but he made me understand that someone had broken his aunt's beloved harp, an heirloom passed down from her mother or grandmother—the exact chain of custody was unclear. Someone had knocked it over and cracked the frame in such a way that it couldn't be repaired, or else would cost a fortune to repair.

"But it wasn't me!" Wyatt shouted.

Out of the corner of my eye, I saw the CO take a step forward. Wyatt must have seen it, too, because he managed to bring himself back in a heartbeat.

Apparently, the aunt had confronted Wyatt in the kitchen, and in the process she'd come up with some colorful terms for his mental handicap. Overwhelmed by the injustice of it all, or maybe just to make her stop screaming, he grabbed a carving knife out of the sink and plunged it into her neck.

"Sorry," he said.

"That was a long time ago," I said.

He nodded and looked suddenly sad, even broken. And I knew without asking: he didn't understand that his aunt was dead. He thought she was out there roaming the planet somewhere, holding down a grudge. That was how he made sense of the fact that she hadn't been to visit him in prison. And that made me wonder: did he understand that he was about to die? I remembered looking out at the storm that morning and thinking that if it was my day to die, I couldn't help but read it as some kind of harbinger. I thought of Bill saying only a rare few know exactly when they'll die. I doubted Wyatt was up to answering, but I decided to go ahead and ask.

"I have kind of a tough question," I said. "Do you understand what's happening here? What's going to happen tonight?"

He smiled.

"They're going to give me a shot," he said. "To help me sleep."

"And that makes you happy?"

He nodded again. Sleep was hard to come by, he told me. They shut off the lights before he was tired, and then he would just lie there, listening. There was a lot to listen to on death row at night. There was a guy named Jack who sang nonsense songs for hours on end, and if the guards tried to make him stop, he'd switch to moaning. The cockroaches came out at night, and Cat Two would scrabble around the cell hunting them, and sometimes she'd bring them to Wyatt as presents. The guards, too, were active at night. You could hear their steps on the concrete, and sometimes you could hear them chatting at their station. The shot they were going to give him would make all the noise go away.

I caught Bill looking at me then, pushing me to take this further, make Wyatt understand just how long his sleep would be. But I couldn't do it. I looked back at Bill as if to say, *I'm just a cook*. Besides, I was sure other people had tried. The guards. His fellow inmates. They probably hadn't been too nice about it, either. And even if I managed to make him understand, I couldn't expect any insightful commentary coming back at me. Wyatt might blubber or lash out, but he wasn't going to ease the world's angst about death.

Time to wrap this up, I thought.

"What's your favorite food, Wyatt?"

He smiled again.

"Sometimes they bring me pudding with fruit in it," he said.

"I don't mean here," I said. "I mean in the world. What's your favorite food in the whole world?"

He didn't have to think much about it, and I probably should have guessed. He wanted macaroni and cheese with bits of hot dog mixed in. The hot dog had to be raw: that was the key to the whole recipe. And for me the absurdity just kept mounting, because it turned out I'd come all this way to cook a meal my own Aunt Joan could have managed.

Still, I gave him the warmest smile I could muster. I told him he had something more to look forward to: the biggest bowl of mac, cheese, and raw hot dog he'd ever seen. That sent him into a rapturous fit of the giggles. He must have startled the cat, because it leaped straight across onto my lap and started using my legs for scratching posts. Every muscle in my body drew tight until I realized the animal had been declawed. This was all more than Wyatt could take. He laughed so hard I thought his beard might jump off his face.

"Cat wants you to cook for her, too," he said.

CHAPTER 16

"We can't do this," I told Bill.

"Do what?" he asked.

"Put this shit on TV."

"Why not?"

We were standing in the staff kitchen while the crew set up. No need for the shopping segment when all you're making is mac and cheese. Timmy had slunk off somewhere, most likely to do a line, and I wanted to get my say in before he resurfaced.

"Were you watching in there?" I asked. "The guy's got no frontal lobe. He thinks his aunt is mad at him because he gave her an owie. He thinks he's about to get a treat and a nap."

"So?"

"So they're executing a toddler."

"They'll execute him whether or not we air the episode. Isn't it better the public knows?"

"Look," I said, "I've done some things in my life, and Lord knows I'm not usually one to take the moral high ground, but this is just wrong. TV is big business. We can't use this guy's death to sell laundry detergent and dick pills."

"If that's the only way we can reach the public, then that's exactly what we'll do."

"Reach the public?"

He nodded. For a second I thought he was going to wink. Good luck convincing Bill he was doing anything but God's work. I decided to try another tack.

"You think people will watch a second episode after they've seen this one?"

"What do you mean?"

"Folks might be curious about the inner life of a psychopath, but what we're giving them here is *Old Yeller* with a human dog. I mean, there's a difference between tugging at the heartstrings and taking a chainsaw to them. Not to mention we're going to look awfully damn foolish. We've got a conversation that goes nowhere and a meal a five-year-old could make."

He tossed this around for a while, or at least pretended to.

"I disagree," he said. "What we've got is a sympathetic victim of the system. Wyatt is an illustrative case. It's been illegal to execute the mentally handicapped since 2002, but states get around it by playing with the definition of *handicapped*. In your home state of Texas, an inmate can be considered handicapped if his mental capacities are deemed inferior to the fictional character Lennie from Steinbeck's *Of Mice and Men*. I shit you not."

"Yeah, but wherever Wyatt falls on whatever scale, he's no martyr. He's a goddamned human being."

"And we'll treat him like a human being. Your interactions with him will anchor the show, but we'll talk with mental health experts, prisoners' rights advocates, judges and jurors, district attorneys and correctional officers, state legislators on both sides. We'll force the American people to confront this issue. Your job—Wyatt's job, too—is to seduce the audience, draw them in. By the time we're done, you'll look like a hero for fixing his mac and cheese. We're making democracy here."

Making democracy? I wanted to ask if there was a part of his CV I'd missed. I mean, I saw *Flesh Stalkers*, or at least some of it. Bill didn't exactly run deep like the rivers.

"He giving you trouble again?"

It was Timmy, who seemed to have a special talent for materializing when no one had summoned him.

"No, sir," Bill said. "We were just laying some theoretical groundwork."

"Well, step it up. The crew's about ready," Timmy said.

Then he walked off again.

I looked around. The kitchen was small and low-tech but more than adequate for the task at hand. You could tell the staff had scrubbed it that morning, and the blue-gray paint on the walls still smelled fresh. On the other hand, there's only so much you can do to dress up a room with a drop ceiling and linoleum floors.

The makeup artist came running up with a tub of base.

"You look a little drained, honey," she said.

"Yeah, well . . . ," I said.

I wondered if she'd be making up Wyatt, too. A job's a job, I guess.

There wasn't much to the cooking. I'd thought about using a fancy mustard—a Dijon mixed with burgundy wine, or maybe a Japanese wasabi mustard I favored—but I wasn't making this for myself, and this wasn't the time to expand Wyatt's horizons. He'd want it just like the aunt he murdered used to make it. Good old American cheese straight out of the cellophane. The kind of frankfurters that swell when you cook them. The best I could do was give him a little extra of each.

I lost three rounds of twenty-one to the boom operator while we waited for the mess to finish baking. When I took it out of the oven and set it on the stovetop, it looked exactly the way it was supposed to: bubbling and golden brown. But somehow the sight of it made me sick. I don't mean a little queasy, but all-the-way ill. I couldn't stop myself from imagining the cheese and noodles hardening in Wyatt's gut after his body had stopped digesting. I didn't even know if that was how death worked, but it was what I pictured. I bolted for the hall and puked what was left of the hotel breakfast into a garbage can. A CO stood there watching but didn't say a word. I didn't, either. Not to him or to Bill and the crew when I got back.

"Where's the family?" I asked.

"Family?" Bill said.

"Or friend. Whoever's going to sit with Wyatt while he eats."

"Wyatt doesn't have any friends. His aunt was his only family."

"You checked?"

"His visitor log is a blank. In the fifteen years he's been here, no one has come to see him."

"Jesus Christ," I said. "Isn't there a chaplain or a shrink?"

Bill shook his head. "I asked," he said. "The prison won't authorize it."

"So you're just going to film him eating by himself?"

"What choice do I have?"

I didn't buy it. Cole was behind this somehow. He was capable of great attention to detail when he wanted to hurt a guy. But then that wasn't Wyatt's fault.

"I'll do it," I said. "But not with the cameras. Just me and Wyatt in his cell."

"Not possible," Bill said. "The warden has already forbidden us to film the execution. The show needs some kind of closure. We need his reaction to your meal."

I took off my apron and chef's hat. I'd forgotten I was wearing them. I'd been wearing them the entire time we played cards.

"Fine," I said. "Let's go."

•

I didn't dress up the mac and cheese at all, just dumped the whole pan into a mixing bowl and stuck a spoon in the center. Parsley would have confused Wyatt.

And then there we all were, back in his cell. He seemed curious about why these people with their fancy machines and bright lights were watching him eat, but he didn't have the words to ask, and after a while he stopped noticing them because he really did enjoy his last supper. He held the spoon in his fist and just kept shoveling. A good thousand-calorie meal never made it past his beard, but he was grinning and happy, and he even shared a few noodles with Cat Two.

"Yes," he said when he was done, and that was enough for me.

Otherwise, we didn't exchange a word. I'd been so worried about keeping company with a man during his final moments, but in Wyatt's case it should have been the easiest thing in the world. You could tell he was glad for the company, even if he didn't say much. All I had to do was hold it together. But it's damn hard, knowing the man in front of you is a tragedy about to happen and there's not a thing you can do to change his fate. Somehow it's harder still when the man in question doesn't know himself what's about to happen and there's no way to make him understand. It might be easier for him, but it's harder for you.

I can't say what Wyatt would have been like with all cylinders firing. Maybe he would have been a prick like all the others. Maybe he would have been a high-functioning sociopath—a Moriarty or a Lex Luthor. Or maybe he would have been a churchgoing working stiff who lived for his beer at the end of the day. But whether he was born that way or someone dropped him on his head, Wyatt was pure innocence. He could only ever be innocent, and painting him as some kind of evil that had to be driven from the earth was just a thin disguise for bloodlust. Someone like Slither, sure. I could have watched Slither die at sunset and forgotten about it by bedtime. But not Wyatt. And if I had any kind of victory that day, it was that I managed to shake Wyatt's hand and walk away before my face went crimson and the floodgates opened.

CHAPTER 17

Flying home, it felt like Slither and Wyatt and the others were on the plane with me. Like I was taking the red-eye with my dead. It wasn't just that they'd died with my food in their bellies; it was like I'd stuck the needle in their arms. Like I'd been there egging them on at every wrong turn, shouting down their good angels. Like the people they'd killed and their own deaths were part of a far-ranging scheme to get my own TV show. Because even if I hadn't asked for any of it, even if I didn't want it now, even if I was just going where life took me, I was sure as shit profiting off a whole lot of misery, starting with my own kid brother.

Sitting there on that dark plane, I tried like hell to trace it all back, like I'd woken up in someone else's life and was searching out my bearings. And I kept finding myself at the same starting point: my first job for Cole.

•

About a week after that incident with the senator, Ryan and I came home from school on a half-day to find a construction crew dismantling Aunt Joan's shack. There was a Dumpster out front beside a pickup with "Grant's Remodeling" emblazoned on the side. A gaggle of dusty-looking men carried things into and out of the house. I didn't know who to approach or what to ask, but then Cole pulled up in his Jaguar, and my questions were more or less answered before he got out.

"A chef needs a kitchen," he said, winking.

He probably thought I'd explode with gratitude right there, but mostly I was suspicious. We hadn't been to the rec center since that night. I wouldn't let Ryan go. After the beating Cole had given the senator's muscle, I was scared. Scared because I had an idea he'd staged it for us, but I had no idea why.

"And every kid needs a home," he added. "I stopped by here the other day and peeked in the window. No real reason. I was in the neighborhood and curious. You kids can't live like this. I can't say goodbye to you at night knowing that this is where you lay your heads."

I watched the workers carry misshapen and mouse-tattered boxes out of the house and heave them into the Dumpster. Boxes that hadn't been opened in all the time Ryan and I lived there.

"Does Aunt Joan know?" I asked.

"It's a surprise," he said.

Ryan slapped his forehead with his palm, which was kind of a funny gesture coming from a nine-year-old.

"Hold on," Cole said. "I want to show you something."

He fetched a long scroll of paper from the trunk and unfurled it across the hood. A pale-gray blueprint drawn in solid black and dotted navy lines. He patted Ryan's head and pointed to a rectangle in the top right corner.

"How would you like your own room?" he asked.

Ryan smiled and kind of hopped in place.

"I thought as much," Cole said. "Granted, it won't be large. There's only so much we can do with limited space, but it will have plenty of bells and whistles. What do you think of a bed made up to look like a boxing ring?"

Ryan threw some shadow punches. Cole was his best friend again.

"Now, for your kitchen," Cole said. "I'm amazed that stove in there works at all."

He started talking about black slate countertops, a fridge with two doors, a microwave and dishwasher, an overhead rack for top-shelf pots and pans.

"Again," he said, "the space is limiting. I would have loved to build you an island."

I found it all kind of hard to picture, but then Ryan and I hadn't been given so much as a Christmas present since our parents died, and I knew what Cole was offering would be more than I could resist—more than I could ask Ryan to resist. The high road is too far to travel when you're piss-poor with no prospects. And that goes double when you've only just turned fourteen.

He took us on a tour and told us what else he planned to change. He was going to give us what he called a proper bathroom because the one we had now was barely an indoor outhouse. The plumbing didn't work a lick. What water dribbled out of the showerhead was dirt-brown, and half the time when you turned it on an army of tiny bugs came scurrying from the nozzle. The toilet couldn't handle more than a pebble-sized turd, and there wasn't any sink at all: we had to brush our teeth in the kitchen. As much as possible, Ryan and I did our shitting at school and our showering at Austin Rec.

So who was I to say no? I was young and inexperienced, but I wasn't starry-eyed. I knew there'd be a price somewhere down the line, and I was pretty sure Cole already knew what that price would be. But sometimes in life you have to put off thinking about the consequences. That's as true now as it was then.

By the time Aunt Joan got home, the small but efficient crew had transferred a few decades' worth of hoarding from house to Dumpster. She saw what was happening, saw us standing out front, dropped her sack of canned goods, and came running. Somehow she knew to go straight for Cole. He squared up and braced himself. I'd never heard her voice hit that volume before. I'd never heard it for that long at one stretch before. Her face turned hypertension red, and she'd have clawed Cole to a pulp if he hadn't grabbed both her wrists. Ryan retreated to the other side of the Jaguar. Grant's construction crew stopped and gawked. I just stood watching, waiting to see what Cole would do.

Aunt Joan tried to break away and start for the house, but Cole held firm.

"Listen, darling," he said, but that was all she'd let him get out. She called him a son of a whore and a bunch of other things that went by too fast for me to catch. It struck me, though, that she knew exactly who he was. I heard her mention the rec center, and I heard her accuse him of slinging dope and a slew of other things I still didn't want to believe he'd done. It made me wonder if they'd had dealings before, or if the adults in town all knew one another the way the kids at school did.

Cole, for his part, seemed to like the recognition. He just smiled and kept holding her until she ran out of gas, which took longer than I would have thought. Then he pulled her off to the side and talked to her in a low voice, and whatever he said did the trick, because she turned that frown around in record time. My educated guess is that he named her poison of choice and said she had a pipeline for as long as she wanted. Which would make sense, because the quality of her stupors seemed to pick up in the following weeks. She drooled less in her sleep, and her little moans suggested she was off somewhere good—maybe lying on a beach in Cancun or sunning herself in a meadow rich with wildflowers.

•

We couldn't stay in the house while they were fixing it up, but Cole had thought of that, too. He put us up at a four-star hotel downtown, in a suite with adjoining rooms. He told us to order whatever we wanted from room service and gave me two hundred dollars in cash for tipping.

I won't lie: we had a blast, and images of that campaign manager writhing around on the floor faded pretty quick. Our room had two queen-size beds in it, whereas at home we shared a single twin, and the bathroom was about a 1,000 percent upgrade. Ryan opened all the little soaps and shampoos and conditioners and sniffed them one by one.

"We're going to smell like flowers," he said.

"There are worse things," I told him, then took his arm and pulled him over to the window. We were on a high floor, and while there wasn't much to look at in terms of skyline or landscape, neither of us had been able to see so far before.

"This is going to be the best spring break ever," Ryan said.

"Yeah," I said. "We'll have something to write about this year."

We stood staring for a bit and then took to jumping back and forth between the two beds. When our breath ran out, I grabbed some Cokes and candy bars from the mini-fridge, and we switched on the TV. Ryan was mesmerized by the sheer number of channels. At first he couldn't seem to stick to any one for longer than a heartbeat, but as the week wore on he started to show a clear preference for anything involving law enforcement. It was around this time that he started to take himself seriously as a boxer, and one afternoon I watched him jab, cross, bob, and weave his way through four hours of a *Cops* marathon.

We barely saw Aunt Joan all week. The Do Not Disturb sign hung in perpetuity from her door, and it wasn't hard to imagine what she might be doing in there. Meanwhile, Ryan and I explored. A hotel is like a universe all its own when you're a kid. Especially a large hotel. For an entire afternoon we just wandered the halls pretending we were inside the Death Star, arguing over which of us got to be Han Solo and which of us had to be Luke.

We didn't step foot outside all week. We didn't need to. Pick up the phone and they'd bring you just about anything you wanted. At first when I called I tried to make my voice sound deep and adult, but Ryan laughed at me, and I could tell the room service operators didn't much care. They'd have brought me alcohol if I asked, but I'd promised Cole I wouldn't, and he was footing the bill. One night I ordered the seafood sampler and made Ryan taste fried squid and baked clam and raw oyster. Sometimes I think my forcing things on him too young is why his taste buds never developed.

There was an Olympics-size pool in the basement, nicer even than the one at the rec center, and most days after breakfast there was just me and Ryan in it. That pool was where I had what I consider my sexual awakening. I'd had fantasies before, but mostly I still thought girls were gross, and it was only recently that I'd stopped shooting blanks. The morning lifeguard couldn't have

been more than four or five years older than me, and the bikini she
wore revealed parts I'd never seen in person. We'd stay until her
shift ended, whether or not Ryan wanted to, and for hours afterward I couldn't keep myself from thinking about her stomach: flat
and soft, with a touch of down around the belly button and a fine
layer of mist from the pool. Now and again she'd lay a hand across
it, and somehow that gesture made me aware of some new thing
inside me, something hell-bent on busting out.

But what I remember most about that week was a question Ryan
asked me one night just after I switched off the lights.

"James," he asked, "how come we don't have any friends?"

I told him to shut his eyes and be quiet, but he'd given me something to chew on in the dark for hours to come, because even then
I had a hard time sleeping. At first I was offended. I figured he was
bored of me and wanted someone his own age to play with. But
then I gave it some real thought, and the more I mulled it over, the
more I realized how strange it was that I'd never thought about it
before. I wasn't opposed to having friends; I just didn't care much
one way or the other. And it was this not caring I couldn't wrap my
mind around. Where did it come from? I had a feeling like I knew
in my gut but not my brain. There was something that predated
the not caring—some deep-seated belief. A conviction, even, that it
wasn't possible for us to make friends. And since it wasn't possible, I
didn't let myself want it. I learned to like things the way they were.
Or maybe I just never learned *not* to like them.

But why? Why didn't I want to be popular like every other kid?
The obvious answer had to do with Aunt Joan and that hovel we
lived in. When you make friends, you have to be prepared to bring
them home, and I couldn't see myself rolling Aunt Joan off the couch
so me and my buddies could watch the game.

I held that thought and kind of tried it on for a while, but it felt
more easy than true. I worked backward to my parents. Was there
something about them—about their death—that made me a loner?
And I realized I couldn't think about them without Ryan's face floating
into the picture. He was what I had left of them. By looking after him,
I was keeping them alive. And that's when I hit on the thought that

did feel true: if I reached out to other people, then I'd lose Ryan. And if I lost Ryan, I'd be by myself in a way I could never fix.

Without putting words to it, I'd always just assumed Ryan felt the same. There was me and him, and then there was the world outside of me and him. But he didn't feel the same. His question proved it. He was craving a wider circle, and that left me feeling all-the-way hollowed out. Even now, looking back, I feel sorry for myself in that moment, and I can't say the same of any other moment in my life. It was then I understood for the first time that Ryan and I were two different people, and that sooner or later we'd both have to go it alone.

Exactly one week after we checked in, Cole sent word the crew was done. He came to pick us up himself. We were sad to go, and I already had ideas about sneaking in to visit my lifeguard crush. But watching the city-style buildings scroll by through the car window, I had a feeling that downtown Austin was being erased, kind of like the story about the bird eating the bread crumb trail: I'd never be able to find my way back.

Aunt Joan fell asleep in the front passenger seat, and no one bothered to wake her when we pulled up to the house. Cole gave Ryan and me a private tour.

"The crew had to delay construction for forty-eight hours so an exterminator could come in and bomb the place," he said. "Other than that, it all went as planned."

He opened the door and waved us inside. In a neighborhood where the houses all looked like lunch boxes, I thought at first we'd walked into the wrong one. It wasn't a question of what was different: I couldn't find a single thing that was the same. With the mounds of trash gone, the place felt palatial. The wood floors were gleaming now, and the walls were all new colors. In place of Aunt Joan's duct-taped futon was a charcoal-gray sectional with footrests at either end, and in place of the shoebox-sized black-and-white TV, there was a screen large enough to fit all three of our reflections at once.

"Holy shit," Ryan said.

"Easy now," Cole said. "Let's move on to the kitchen."

It was exactly like he'd described it when we were looking at the blueprint, only I couldn't see it then. In person, every line was clean and sleek. Black slate countertops complemented a ceramic-tile backsplash; a full set of cast-iron pots and pans hung from a silver overhead rack; buttons on the microwave promised to do everything short of the food shopping; and the stainless-steel refrigerator made its own water and ice.

Ryan, anxious to see his new room, yawned his way through this part of the tour, but I couldn't keep my jaw from hanging open.

"Do you see yourself cooking here?" Cole asked.

I said I did, but I didn't—not yet. Cole pulled one of the two refrigerator doors open.

"Take a look," he said.

Besides core ingredients like eggs and milk and butter, there were a dozen different kinds of cheese, a half dozen kinds of mushrooms, bunches of tarragon and sage and rosemary, a glass bottle of fresh-squeezed orange juice, packages of tofu ranging from silken to extra firm, a small basket filled with lemons and limes.

I switched to the freezer side, found cuts of beef, chicken breasts wrapped in butcher paper, whole salmon and snapper and pike.

"You'll have fun exploring the cabinets, too," Cole said.

"But first my room," Ryan said.

"I tell you what," Cole said. "Why don't you run ahead and check it out?"

He didn't have to ask twice. When we were alone, Cole put a hand on my shoulder.

"So what do you think?" he asked.

I couldn't come up with anything better than "Amazing."

"Of course, cooking takes money," he said. "But I have work for you, too."

"Anything," I said. "I'll do dishes, bus tables, prep salads. Just tell me when I start."

"You have to be sixteen to work in a restaurant," he said. "For now, I'm thinking more in terms of errands."

"What kinds of errands?" I asked.

He reached up under his shirt, which he'd left untucked for once, and pulled a thick manila folder from his waistband.

"Deliveries," he said. "Again, for now."

I knew better than to ask what I'd be delivering.

"All right," I said, taking the envelope.

"Excellent," Cole said. "I'll write out the address and directions. Now, why don't you go fetch your aunt. We'll show her the new bathroom."

Looking back, the cynical part of me says Cole was grooming us, reeling us in. But he must have loved us, too. There has to be a way for both things to be true.

Not that it matters now.

CHAPTER 18

"Takeout?" Cheryl said. "You feeling under the weather?"

"Everybody needs a break once in a while."

"From cooking? I would have thought you'd take a break from breathing first."

I shrugged.

"Chinese?" I asked.

"Kung pao shrimp," she said. "Extra hot."

I called it in, opened a bottle of wine, then sat with her on her sofa—the same futon she'd used as a bed all through college and law school. That was one of the things I loved about Cheryl. Ten years into her career and she was maybe the most sought-after defense attorney in all of Texas. She had about fifty thousand dollars' worth of original artwork on her walls, but you'd have thought she furnished her condo out of a thrift shop. Cheryl knew what mattered to her, and she barely noticed what didn't.

"Why don't we eat at Companion anymore?" she asked.

"We haven't eaten there in a few weeks," I said. "That doesn't mean we don't eat there anymore."

"You're sure nothing's going on?" she asked. "With the restaurant?"

"Like I said, everyone needs a break once in a while."

"I was afraid maybe something happened to Louis and you were keeping it from me."

The time had come. I hated lying to Cheryl, but what choice did I have?

"Louis decided to chase a dream before it was too late. That's all."

"Buenos Aires?"

I nodded.

"And that's not some euphemism, like the rainbow bridge?"

"Rainbow bridge?"

"Where the dead dogs go."

"Louis is alive," I told her. "At least as far as I know."

Of course it crossed my mind that Cheryl tore apart liars for a living.

"Fine," she said. "It's probably better that we meet here anyway. I've got big news. News that needs to stay between us for now."

"What kind of news?"

"I found a hole. In Ryan's case. Or it found me. Just came traipsing into the office around lunchtime. Good thing I eat at my desk."

"A hole came walking into your office?"

"One I found very credible, though I'm not sure a judge will."

"Enough with the tease," I said.

"All right. Ryan wasn't alone when he shot that officer. Or maybe I should say 'when that officer was shot.'"

She had every scrap of my attention. I sat up a little straighter, nodded for her to go on.

"A witness came forward. A nineteen-year-old kid who claims he was in the garage under Ryan's apartment when the shooting happened. More importantly, he claims he heard voices *after* the shot was fired. Two male voices."

"He's sure it wasn't just Ryan talking to himself?"

"Positive. One of the voices was hysterical, the other deep and calm."

I was starting to feel like an athlete who knew he'd lost but was stuck playing out the rest of the game.

"So why'd this kid come forward now?" I asked. "Why not during the trial? And where was he when the cops showed up?"

"Well, that's the rub," Cheryl said. "Nicholas may have been tres-passing at the time. And he may have a little bit of a meth problem."

"Don't tell me he was robbing the place."

"It's a little more complicated than that. Nicholas and his father are estranged. His father was Ryan's landlord. Nicholas claims he came back for some piece of memorabilia—a trophy from his high school football days."

"That's a little thin," I said. "Even for a junkie."

"I know it sounds that way. He's not the most polished witness, but I believe him. Which is why I need your help."

"My help?"

"Look, the kid's not asking for anything. He claims his conscience got the better of him. But you're right: no judge will give him the time of day. If his story is true, it means Ryan's been protecting someone. I need to know who. And if Ryan hasn't told me by now, then he isn't going to."

"You want me to ask him?" I said.

She gave me a look that was half coy, half commanding.

"Unless you already know," she said.

And there it was: the first whiff of suspicion.

"I'll have the warden set up a conjugal," I said.

•

"So she knows?" Ryan asked.

"She suspects."

We were eating lamb stew from Pascal's, the shop Cole took us to all those years ago before he had me make dinner for the senator. I didn't have the heart or energy to bake one myself, and stew is the perfect meal for Ryan because all the ingredients sit right there in the same bowl. If he noticed it wasn't my cooking he didn't say anything, and circumstances aside, that stung a little.

"So what are you going to do?" he asked.

I shrugged.

"What can I do?"

"Well," he said, "we know he's my ex-landlord's kid. We know he uses. He can't be that hard to find."

"And then what?"

"Make him understand the value of silence."

"Cole's old line. No, thanks. At some point you've got to let go of the shovel and stop digging your own grave."

"So you just wait? See how it plays out?"

I nodded.

"Could be you end up in here with me."

"Could happen anyway," I said. "Our deal still stands, you know. If Cheryl can't get you off death row, I'll come forward."

"And get a needle in your arm for defending me?"

"I only thought I was defending you."

I watched it play out again in my mind. Me peering through the screen door, seeing a man in a plaid shirt train his gun on my brother. I figured he was one of Cole's, settling the nephew's account. I pulled my piece—the unregistered duplicate, the way Cole had taught me—and stepped inside. The man spun. I fired. It was that simple. Even if I did spend the next week spewing my guts out.

Ryan cut into a chunk of meat with the side of his fork. I'd been too worked up to notice before, but he'd lost weight. A lot of weight.

"I got a better idea," he said.

"What's that?"

"Bring me something. Poison, a knife, a belt. It doesn't matter. I can't get shit in here anymore."

"What are you talking about?"

He dropped his fork, leaned back in his chair.

"Listen," he said, "what the hell are we fighting for? The chance to spend more days in here? My life's a bust. Whether it ends tonight or forty years from now, my tombstone will read the same. All I need—"

"Knock it off," I said. "Just stop."

He reached across, grabbed my forearm.

"It's all right," he said. "It's what I want. And if I'm gone, people stop looking. You're out from under. Free and clear."

I shook my head. I still hadn't filled him in on my new arrangement with Cole.

"I don't give a shit about that," I said.

"You should. I don't believe in heaven or hell, and I'll take decades of nothing over what I got now."

I saw it then. He wasn't just thin; he was tired. The kind of tired you don't recover from in a night or two. The bags under his eyes had spread until he looked like one big bruise.

"What's going on?" I asked.

He smiled.

"I want to die," he said. "I want to die, I'm on death row, and I'm still alive. That's life in a nutshell, ain't it?"

"It's that CO," I said. "I thought he'd laid off."

Ryan held his arms out to the sides.

"You see any bruises?"

"Don't hide shit from me, Ryan," I said. "Not now."

He didn't make it easy, but in the end I got a detailed account. Don, the CO, hadn't laid a finger on him, as per my agreement with Cole, but he found other, more inventive ways to torture my brother. One afternoon Ryan was taken out for his hour in the yard and came back to find his mattress soaked in urine. Ron showed up moments later.

"Jesus Christ," he said. "You've got a toilet right over there. I'd send you to the hole, but it's all booked up—kind of like a resort. So I guess we'll just have to take the mattress."

Ryan watched him haul it out. He didn't glare, didn't say a word. Just stood with his back to the wall and his hands in his pockets. If Ron wanted to beat him again, he'd have to do it without an excuse.

Then he started to mess with Ryan's food. The first time, Ryan took the lid off his tray to find his dinner already eaten—nothing left but chicken bones and white bread crust. Next morning, he found maggots in his Rice Krispies and gasoline in his milk. Then his scrubs came back unlaundered, dirtier than when he'd handed them in, stained with shit and stinking of cigarettes. A day later, the soap and toilet paper disappeared from his cell.

"It's Cole, ain't it?" he said. "Getting revenge for what I did to his nephew. The thing of it is, if I'd known Cole was going to get out, I'd have waited, left his money alone, and gone straight at him."

I guess we can't control how our minds work—because listening to him just then, I felt a surge of anger it took all of me to beat back.

If he hadn't set out to rob Kenny, and if he hadn't killed him in the process, our lives would have carried on, nice and simple. No death row. No *Last Supper*. Cooking would mean what it had always meant. But then, I could hear Ryan saying, there'd be no Companion. I'd probably still be working as a line cook somewhere. And Ryan's addiction would have taken him to a place just as bad.

"I'll fix this," I told him. "You hang tight."

•

I drove from Huntsville right back to Companion. I knew Cole would be there, taking his nightcap the way Louis used to. He was there every night now, and more and more he had other people with him. He was starting to conduct business at that table by the window—real business, like he had thoughts of going legit. I didn't know the details, but he was meeting with real-estate types—developers and contractors and brokers and attorneys—wining and dining them night in and out at my expense. I thought about that and I thought about my brother sitting on a concrete floor picking maggots from his breakfast cereal. I kept myself good and angry all through the three-plus-hour drive. And then I threw open the doors to Companion, thinking I'd grab Cole by the throat and tell him to do his worst from hell.

But I was in for a surprise. A sign on the door read "Closed for a private event." Inside, I found a small film crew (seemed I couldn't get away from them) set up at the bar, their lenses trained on Cole as he spoke very earnestly with an attractive female reporter I recognized from the local news. Cole saw me, waved me over in the middle of his interview. Max looked to be the only employee on duty.

"James," Cole yelled out, smiling like there was nothing but warmth between us. "Come join the party."

He'd dyed his hair jet-black and was wearing a double-breasted suit. I had to give him this much: he looked ten years younger.

"This is Lily Crace, of Channel 9 news," he said. "She's doing a piece on my latest philanthropic endeavor. But then I imagine the two of you know each other. In addition to being the proprietor of this fine establishment, James is a fellow television personality."

He was talking more than he needed to, smiling more intensely than he needed to, and I understood why: he'd seen my face when I walked in, and he knew what was on my mind. He was heading me off at the pass. *Follow my lead*, he was saying. *Play along, and we'll talk later.*

Fuck that, I thought. I was in the mood to blow things up.

"We haven't met, but I'm a big fan," Lily said.

"Likewise," I lied. "So what's this philanthropic endeavor?"

"Mr. Cole is funding a new recreation center."

"I made a donation, that's all," Cole corrected.

"A substantial donation."

"I wish I could do more," Cole said. "I no longer have the energy to run a place that size."

"So this is like a citizen-of-the-month story?" I asked.

"We call it our Citizen Spotlight," Lily said.

"Well, fuck me," I said. "Oh, I'm sorry. I'm probably not supposed to curse."

"We're just talking for now," Lily said. "We can edit later."

"You really don't mind if I join you?"

"I'd be delighted," she said.

"All right, then."

I took the stool between them, thinking, *In for a penny* . . . One of the cameramen hopped to the other side of the bar. Max brought me a kir. I pushed it back, asked for a double bourbon.

"So how do the two of you know each other?" Lily asked.

"James came walking into Austin Rec one day after school . . . what, twenty-two, twenty-three years ago now? That's the remarkable thing about a good rec center: we never advertised, but the kids who needed it most found us. James was a star. He wasn't just hiding from his home life. He took full advantage of the place."

"I came in with my brother," I said. "The one who's on death row. The one who killed Cole's nephew. So, you know, not all success stories."

I took a generous swallow of bourbon, saw I'd set off a faint twitch in Cole's left eyebrow. Lily did her best to look unfazed.

"If one in a thousand is like James, then it's all worth it," Cole said.

"So is it fair to say you had a hand in raising Austin's top chef and TV personality?" Lily asked Cole. She ignored me like she was already looking ahead to the edited segment.

Cole gave a false-modest head tilt. "He learned to cook at Austin Rec."

"Really?" Lily asked.

I made my voice cheery, put on a big grin. "Sure," I said. "Cole raised me and my brother. He had a hand in raising his nephew, too, though mostly that just involved posting bail. Cole raised everyone but his own son. Cole Jr. wants nothing to do with him. Of course, this was all before Cole went away for killing his best friend's wife."

Lily took a sip of ginger ale to hide her blush. I slammed what was left of my bourbon, gestured for another.

"Oh, I'm sorry," I said. "That probably doesn't fit with the piece. Well, like you said, you can always edit later."

"Only because your commentary is unwittingly repetitive," Cole said. "We covered my incarceration before you got here. The state clearly determined they'd arrested the wrong person, or they never would have let me go."

"So they overturned your sentence?" I asked, knowing full well they hadn't.

"That would have meant admitting their mistake," Cole said. "No, they invoked some absurd law whereby I had to admit my guilt in order to be set free."

"An Alford plea," Lily said.

"Yes. So that I can't sue the state."

"Did you plead guilty to fucking Paul's wife?" I asked.

"That never happened."

"Funny how he turned up dead just after you were sent away."

"More tragic than funny," Cole said. "The only funny part was that people blamed me for his death, too, when clearly I was indisposed."

"Well, a shotgun to the back of the head always was your style."

"You're drunk," Cole said. "This is getting tedious."

It's true the bourbon had hit me hard, but I wasn't feeling sloppy. If anything, my senses were heightened, like the world was coming in a little too sharp. I thought of Ryan again, saw him lying in soiled clothes on a concrete floor, unable to wash himself or even wipe his ass, his mind racing, wondering what Cole's stooge had in store for him next.

"Tedious doesn't begin to describe it," I said.

"I'm sensing this isn't the best time," Lily said.

I'd had enough.

"Those are some keen journalistic instincts," I said. "Where were they when you picked a homicidal drug kingpin for your Citizen Spotlight?"

"What the hell is wrong with you?" Cole asked.

I couldn't tell if Max was grinning or grimacing. I kept working on Lily.

"Time for you to pack up and get the fuck out," I said. "Shut that fucking camera off. Shut it off. This is my place, and I didn't give you permission to be here. And I sure as shit didn't sign any release form, so I'd be real careful about who sees this footage."

Cole was reining himself in hard.

"I apologize," he said. "I should have asked." He turned to Lily. "I'm so very sorry. I didn't think this through. Maybe we can talk another time? I'd be happy to come to your studio."

With the camera off, Lily was a lot less pleasant.

"This was a one-shot deal," she said. "I've got a dozen other candidates lined up. One of them is a food critic."

"I'm quaking," I said.

Max walked Lily and her crew to the door. I told him to take off: I'd finish closing myself.

"You broke our deal," I said to Cole when we were alone.

"Deal? I don't have any deal with you; you have a deal with me."

"I saw Ryan today."

"Is that what this is about? Some harmless pranks?"

"Tell your CO to back the fuck off."

Cole grinned. I almost admired his restraint. Younger Cole would have gone for my jugular right there.

"You made a very large mistake tonight," he said. "I'm going home to decide what your punishment will be. You'll know it when it comes, though it won't necessarily come from me, and it may not be delivered to you. Enjoy the rest of your evening."

I watched him walk away and thought to myself, *At least you were smart enough to leave your gun in the car.*

CHAPTER 19

From then on, things started to move fast. A week later, *Last Supper* sent me to Kentucky. Same drill: identical car, swank hotel, garage in the sticks, multiple takes of me driving through the gates. The inmate was an obese pediatrician who'd used his girth to smother a twelve-year-old girl with Down syndrome. He called it a mercy killing.

The pediatrician had strong ideas about his last meal. He wanted traditional Kentucky cuisine: lemon pepper lamb fries with a heaping plate of bourbon balls for dessert. For the uninitiated, lamb fries are testicles. You slice them in half and fry them in vegetable oil. Beyond that, this guy had real specific instructions. The chili peppers had to be Armenian, and the lemon juice had to be fresh-squeezed—nothing from a bottle. Only heirloom tomatoes would do, and he swore if he saw a hint of onion he'd make me start over from scratch.

Like I said before, I'm not squeamish. If anything, I've always enjoyed making the more exotic dishes. From tongue to toes, there's no part of an animal I haven't boiled or sautéed. But standing over a skillet of spitting sheep balls with the cameras staring me down, I felt light-headed, like I might actually pass out. It wasn't the smell or the sight or even the popping sound: it was the overwhelming sense that I was killing this man by cooking for him, like if I refused he'd somehow live to a ripe old age. I knew this was nonsense, but the more I tried to talk myself out of it, the more real the idea became. Like instead of lamb testicles I was frying up a batch of pentobarbital, simmering it down so it would all fit in the needle. Like instead of his chef, I was his judge, jury, and executioner.

So what if you are? I told myself. *He killed a child.*

But that wasn't the point. In my mind, I had the power to stop his death by withholding the thing that's supposed to keep us alive: food. If I turned off the burners and threw the whole mess in the trash, then the child-smotherer would live. Rational or not, it was that simple. But I wouldn't do it. I wouldn't do it because Cole had Louis's fake letters. Because he had pictures of me with a shovel and a body at a shut-down construction site. Because he knew where to find Ryan whenever he wanted. Because I still had Cheryl and Companion and a luxury condo and a life I wasn't ready to let go of. So the fat man had to die, and it might as well be me killing him.

•

Three days later, I was back at home, or rather back at Cheryl's home. I tried to steer us to her place as much as possible because I was still walking around with Cole's threat front and center in my mind. Whatever punishment he decided on, I didn't want Cheryl around when it happened. For the time being, I stalled by telling her I'd killed a black widow in my bathtub and the fumigator couldn't come around for another week. Spiders are the only creature I know for sure Cheryl's afraid of. It's a phobia, really. Once, a tiny green one came spiraling down in front of her while she was driving, and we had a near-death experience on the highway. Throw a poisonous variety into any excuse or alibi and you can be sure she won't look too closely.

So we were at her place, unwinding before bed, sitting on her college futon and sharing a scotch while we played a fourth round of Scrabble. She'd just laid *quixotic* down on a triple word score and ruined my chances of finishing less than a hundred points behind. She was so happy with that one, she took out her phone and snapped a picture. Then she went back to chattering all through my turn, asking me if I'd read *Don Quixote* or seen *Man of La Mancha*. It didn't help that the jazz album on in the background sounded like the sax player was searching for notes only a dog could hear. I was about to concede the game when she said, "It was Kentucky you just went to, right?"

I said it was.

"Hold on," she told me. "I've got to show you something."

She darted out of the room and came back carrying a fold of newspaper.

"Did you hear about this?" she asked, handing it over, tapping an article in the upper right corner. The headline would have made me weak-kneed if I'd been standing:

TWELVE DEAD IN KENTUCKY PRISON
DRUG SCANDAL

"Holy shit," I said.

"Well, your guy can't be one of them, right? I mean, he was already dead."

I shushed her, which meant I'd be in trouble, but I didn't care. My mind and eyes were jumping around too fast for me to read the article straight through. I skimmed first for my name, then for any mention of *Last Supper*. When I didn't find either, I went back to the top and started sorting out the details. Somehow a bad batch of heroin made its way into the prison. Twelve inmates were dead and twelve more had been transported to a secure wing of a local hospital.

I felt some relief, but it was the safe-for-now kind of relief that only carries you for a heartbeat. After that, my mind cut straight to tallying the dead. My dead. Because the bodies were piling up, and it didn't much matter if I'd pulled the trigger or dug the grave or cooked the last meal. Just like it didn't matter if I knew the drugs were poisoned. People were dropping all around me, and my plausible deniability was starting to wear real thin. After a while, you've got to quit saying *This would have happened with or without me*. Probably I should have stopped a long time ago.

I must have lost my color, because Cheryl asked, "Hey, are you all right?"

I shook my head.

"I'm feeling a little beat," I said. "I think I'm going to call it a night. Looks like you've got the game won anyway."

She looked me up and down.

"You sure you're just tired?" she asked. "You didn't know any of those inmates, did you?"

"No," I said, "I didn't. But I am tired, and I have to be at the restaurant early tomorrow."

"Uh-oh," she said. "That's your I'm-sleeping-at-home voice. I was going to bring you breakfast in bed."

"Rain check?"

"Fair enough. But you never told me what Ryan said. I was going to ask in the morning, keep tonight about us."

"Right," I said. "I almost forgot. He didn't say anything. I mean, he was alone. He doesn't know what the landlord's kid is talking about."

"Fuck," she said.

•

Of course, I wasn't really going home. I was going to look for Cole. I kept remembering what he'd said: *You'll know it when it comes, though it won't necessarily come from me, and it may not be delivered to you.*

I saw it in that article. That was Cole reminding me the stakes were as high as he chose to make them. It was Cole reminding me what he was capable of, like I might have forgotten.

It was just after ten o'clock, and if I hurried I could still catch him at Companion. In the aftermath of his spoiled TV debut he'd doubled down, decided to mark his territory, or mark my territory as his. He was at Companion nonstop now, running up a tab he had no intention of paying off, sampling everything on the menu, including the hundred-dollar bottles of wine. He even worked there afternoons now, whatever work meant for him, staking out a small table or a corner of the bar, opening his brand-new laptop and looking busy, though I'd guess he spent most of his time playing solitaire like any good ex-con. The staff took a liking to him because he demanded little and tipped at the 40 percent mark, though those tips also went on his tab.

No doubt about it: I smelled a coup coming. Cole had designs on Companion, but that was more than I could worry about just then. I was focused on the dead. On Cole's nephew and Ryan's cop. On Louis. On Slither and Wyatt and the obese pediatrician. On the twelve Kentucky inmates who thought they were just getting high, taking a little break from the life they'd backed themselves into. I was stuck in the notion that all those deaths were linked to my cooking. Not like I'd killed them, but like my cooking itself invited death.

There was only one way I could think of to rescind that invitation, and that was to sacrifice myself. Give myself over to Cole completely. *My wish is your command, sir. Let's just keep the killing to a minimum.* In other words, placate him. Make him believe I'd seen the error of my ways. Make him believe I was fourteen again and he was my personal savior. Give him no more reason to flex. At least for now.

At that time of night, there wasn't much traffic to get in my way. I floored it whenever I could and was closing in on the parking lot when my phone fired up a chorus of James Brown's "Prisoner of Love." That was the ringtone I'd assigned to Warden Ottie Woodrell, mostly to amuse myself, because the warden was carrying a little torch for me and did a piss-poor job of hiding it. Still, she'd never made a declaration, and she'd never called me this late before, so I figured whatever had her calling now had to be code red. I pulled in front of a fire hydrant and dug out my phone.

"Hello, James," Ottie said, and I could tell already I was in for bad news because there wasn't a hint of flirtation in her voice.

"You're working late tonight," I said, trying to sound casual.

"I was called in," she said. "There's been an incident. It involves Ryan."

"What kind of incident?"

"We're still investigating, but it seems he got into an altercation with a guard."

"Altercation?"

"He attacked one of our correctional officers with a shank."

Now, I knew that was bullshit. Ryan had nothing to make a shank from. No toothbrush, no mattress coils. Nothing.

"How bad is my brother hurt?" I asked.

"His right arm is broken. His face is badly bruised, and they had to wire his jaw shut."

"Jesus Christ."

"It seems he fell face forward onto a concrete floor. On the plus side, X-rays were negative for internal damage. He should be right as rain in three to four weeks."

So he'll look pretty when you kill him, I thought.

"I want to see Ryan," I said. "Now."

"I told you, he's in the infirmary. I can't allow a civilian to—"

"Ottie, you're the goddamn warden. You can allow whatever you want."

She hesitated.

"Where are you now?" she asked.

"Austin."

"By the time you got here, it would be . . . what? Two in the morning? Why don't you—"

"I just want to sit with him. I don't care if he knows I'm there."

My brain shifted to bargaining mode. I'd have given her anything she wanted. I'd have slept with her if that was what it took, and Ottie's got two decades on me, not to mention her botched dental surgery.

"You haven't been drinking or anything, have you?" she asked.

"Absolutely not."

She was quiet for a beat, but we both knew she'd already given in.

"All right," she said. "Call me back on this line when you're at the gates. I'll come get you myself."

"Like you said, it'll take me at least three hours."

"I'll nap on the couch in my office."

"God bless you, Ottie," I said.

And then I was back on the road, headed for the highway.

•

I spent all that drive imagining what I'd find at the end of it. I imagined Ryan's face mangled and skinned. I pictured him with an ear ripped off, an eye swollen shut, a row of teeth gone, two lips leaking blood. But none of that prepared me for what I actually saw when I sat down at his bedside.

Cole's flunky had gone as far as he could go without making death row redundant. Ryan's eyes were puffed out like toad throats and had turned colors I didn't know skin could turn. His forehead was one long abrasion, and they'd put some kind of protective covering over the bridge of his nose. He was unconscious, with tubes running out of his nostrils and an IV stuck in his good arm.

Ottie rested a hand on my shoulder, and I let it lie there while I teared up wondering just how much Ryan could take. And at the same time I felt a tinge of relief, because I'd come real close to making a huge mistake. I'd thought there were two ways to deal with Cole, but there was only the one.

I was going to kill that motherfucker. Which is what I should have done the first time he laid hands on Ryan.

CHAPTER 20

That delivery I made for Cole was just the first of many. I never looked inside the envelope—that was against the rules—but I'd heard Cole accused of dealing enough times to put two and two together. This wasn't street-level stuff: the envelope was always small, and the person I handed it off to was always a who's-who-in-Austin type. Ryan came with me because he always came with me, but at the outset, in my mind at least, it was just me working for Cole. Sometimes I delivered right to the customer's doorstep, but more often I'd make the handoff in a parking lot or a diner or a public square.

Cole would give me a time, a location, and a rough description of the buyer. Some of them were famous, or at least Texas famous. One was a lawyer I recognized from his TV commercials—a large, white-haired guy who wore a blue blazer and a big beige Stetson. He didn't try to hide who he was, either. Ryan and I walked right into his office like we were in need of counsel and had an appointment. In his commercials, he made big claims about million-dollar settlements, but his lobby smelled like a strip club and the diplomas in his office all hung crooked in cheap frames. When he died of an overdose a few years later, police found more than two thousand porno cassettes crowding the bookshelves in his bedroom, all alphabetized and kept in the original packaging. I remember Cole saying, *People find all kinds of ways to make a life.*

By the time I was sixteen going on seventeen, Cole moved me off of deliveries and made me what he called his personal caterer. He gave me a regular salary and put me on the Austin Rec payroll. I didn't do much cooking for the center, though. Mostly I made buffets for Cole's backroom card games. Barbecue and potato salad and the occasional fish fry. These were invitation-only events, and with a few exceptions I saw the same faces in different combinations every time. Some of the players were high-end clients I recognized from my deliveries, and none of them thought anything of dropping fifty grand in an hour.

Ryan, who'd just turned thirteen, took over the deliveries. He knew the routes and the customers, and Cole said he was too young to be hanging around illegal card games. Of course, Cole was concerned for the game, not Ryan: he thought some of the legit-businessman players would get their moral hackles up with a barely pubescent kid looking over their shoulders. I could have continued making the deliveries, too, but Cole wanted to give Ryan some responsibility of his own. Meanwhile, he kept grooming Ryan to be muscle, having him learn everything from pugilism to jujitsu, with a healthy dose of firearms training thrown in.

If I'm going to be honest, Cole wasn't a bad boss in those days. As long as you performed, he let you do things your way. No micromanaging, no hand-holding, no second-guessing, and more than a few surprise bonuses. The problem was that Ryan didn't always perform. He was tall and strong and naturally athletic, but he had a lazy streak, and when puberty hit he turned bitter. He figured since life robbed us of our parents and saddled us with Aunt Joan, he was owed something, and that didn't sit well with Cole.

"Your sibling has no drive," Cole complained.

"He's just a kid," I said, which must have sounded strange coming from a sixteen-year-old.

Their rift started innocently enough, with Ryan skipping a sparring session here and there. But then, a little more a year in, he was late for a delivery, and then he missed one altogether. The tipping point came when Cole caught Ryan behind the rec center smoking a joint with a kid he'd just beaten the shit out of in the ring.

"If he wasn't your brother I'd have cut him off a long time ago," Cole said. "So you talk to him while he still has a tongue to talk with. And make sure you stress this point: if he botches another delivery, he's out. With his grades, he's not exactly Harvard-bound, so encourage him to think carefully about his prospects."

Meanwhile, I was inching pretty fast up Cole's corporate ladder. I was running games, not just catering them, and if somebody outside our circle had a business proposal for Cole, he had to run it by me first. The money felt damn good, and at the tender age of eighteen I was getting VIP treatment at restaurants and sporting venues all over town. I was starting to see Ryan as the wild card: the half-rabid, half-narcoleptic teen hell-bent on tanking my future along with his. At fourteen he was taller than me and ten times as agile. He'd become hard as hell to rein in, especially since, as he was fond of pointing out, I wasn't his dad, and neither was Cole. Day in and out I rubbed noses with gangsters two or three times my age, but nothing made my stomach coil like a confrontation with my kid brother.

"You're fucking up, Ryan," I told him. "You need to get it together before the damage can't be undone."

"Cole's a dickhead, and you're his fucking puppet," Ryan said.

"Cole's the only person who's ever done a thing for us."

Ryan got right up in my face.

"Why do you think that is?" he said. "Two little orphan boys living in a shack with their junkie aunt. We were cheap labor. Easy to brainwash. He'd forget we were alive if we stopped being useful."

Looking back now, it's hard to see how I ever got pegged as the smart one. Of course I knew there was truth in what he was saying, but I thought there was more to it. I believed we—and yes, especially me—had the power to break Cole's heart. And I guess I still believe that much, because the vengeance he took on us when he got out was slow and hate-fueled and gave him far too much pleasure.

"Well, maybe you shouldn't stop being useful, then," I said, "because what the hell else do you have going on?"

I saw all the rage in him shoot straight to the surface. He thought about hitting me then. He didn't just want to hit me; he wanted to break me. Leave me in a pile on Aunt Joan's kitchen floor and walk away from all of it. From me. From Cole. From Aunt Joan. From the rec center and Austin and Texas. I don't know why he didn't. I don't know if love trumped hate or if he just realized he had nowhere else to go.

"Fuck you," he said, then ran into his postage stamp of a room and slammed the door.

I stepped to the living room, looked in on Aunt Joan. She was sound asleep, a fat spit bubble rising from her lips.

•

A week later, Ryan failed to show for a delivery, and Cole banished him in no uncertain terms. He issued a gangster-style restraining order: if Ryan came anywhere near the rec center, his next stop would be the emergency room. It embarrasses me now, but at the time I sided with Cole. I thought he was teaching Ryan a valuable lesson. Something about the value of work and commitment.

Just six months after that, three weeks shy of Ryan's sweet sixteen, Aunt Joan died. Ryan found her on the bathroom floor. She'd OD'd, but more than anything she died from not wanting to be alive. That's what the drugs and alcohol were always about for her.

She died intestate, and the bank put a lien on her bungalow. We had to pay up or get out. It wasn't much—just under twenty grand— and I should have had it, but I was young and dumb with my money. I'd paid cash for a brand-new, souped-up F-150, bought an antique hunting rifle even though I didn't hunt, and sunk a bundle into a string of short-lived romances. It wasn't the time to ask Cole for a loan, either. He'd drawn a definitive line between me and Ryan, but it was clear I had my brother's stink on me. And as for working something out with the bank, on paper I only made ten thousand dollars a year: Cole paid out the rest in one-hundred-dollar bills.

Well, a week after that, Ryan walked into my room and handed me a grocery sack filled with bundles of cash totaling $19,500. He turned around and walked out before I'd finished counting. I chased him outside, grabbed his arm, and spun him around. We stood facing each other in the white-gravel yard Cole had installed years ago.

"Get the fuck off me," Ryan said.

"Keep your voice down."

"You're welcome."

"Welcome?"

"Now you can buy this shithole outright."

"Ryan, where did that money come from?"

"My piggy bank."

I considered for a second whether that might be true. Cole had been paying him, too, but until not too long ago that was just an allowance, and Ryan wasn't any better with money than me.

"What did you do, Ryan?"

He gave me a big, sloppy grin. His pupils were the size of quarters, and the whites of his eyes were jagged red.

"Don't you get it?" he said. "We don't need Cole. Anyone with balls can break the law. Why go broke paying a middleman?"

He scared me then. I was scared for him, not of him. I didn't realize how hard he'd become. I let go of his arm, watched him jog off down the block, no doubt on the way to meet his dealer.

It took Cole less than twenty-four hours to figure out what happened. Ryan had robbed one of the high-end clients on his delivery route, a fortysomething trust-fund baby who spent his nights playing western swing in Austin clubs. Ryan was caught on camera pawning a vintage Gibson guitar. Cole, the pawnshop owner, and Ryan's victim came to a mutual agreement.

The hospital called at three in the morning. I almost didn't pick up. EMTs had found Ryan curled in a fetal position on a bus stop bench while running their nightly check on the homeless. The fingers on his right hand were badly dislocated. He had three broken ribs and one shattered kneecap. The internal bleeding might have killed him if the EMTs hadn't rolled by, but then Cole was careful:

he had his men drop Ryan where he'd be found. This was a warning. The absence of head trauma made that much clear.

Ryan was still in the ICU when I got there. He was sedated, curtained off from other patients. When I stepped into his makeshift room, I barely saw him. What I saw instead was Cole sitting at his bedside, sipping from a coffee cup.

"What are you doing here?" I asked.

He looked up, grinned.

"I brought flowers," he said, "but the nurses told me flowers aren't allowed in this wing."

"I thought only family could visit."

"I am family, aren't I?"

I looked down at Ryan. He was sound asleep, with a blanket pulled up to his chin. If it weren't for the IV and the pulse monitor, I wouldn't have known anything was wrong with him.

"Not anymore," I said.

"James—"

"I'm asking you to leave."

He stood, stepped closer to me, spoke in a whisper.

"I just saved us all a much bigger problem," he said. "Sometimes a kid needs to be put in his place."

I made a show of looking around.

"Intensive care?" I said.

"It was that or the morgue."

"How do I know you weren't trying for the morgue?"

"You know."

"Yeah," I said. "But you still have to leave."

"Think this over, James. Your lives become much harder without me."

I sniggered, laid a hand on Ryan's foot.

"So this is the easy version?" I asked.

"This is just a realignment."

I thought about what Ryan said: we were cheap labor, easy to brainwash. But really it was only me Cole had brainwashed.

"I won't be working for you anymore," I said. "I can't. Not now."

He knew I was serious because there wasn't any anger in my voice. There wasn't any emotion in my voice at all. I was acting on principle. Deep down, I wanted Cole to stay. I wanted him to be there when I got married, when I opened my first restaurant, when my wife had our first kid.

"Like I said, think this over. I'll give you some space. But don't take too long."

I watched him walk away, then sat where he'd been sitting. I looked at Ryan, traced his profile with my eyes. He still wasn't sixteen, but already he had college girls chasing after him. I thought about everything that he could be and never would be—and I wondered if the difference was my fault. Because I had no doubts or illusions: Ryan wasn't the type to pan out, and I'd just taken a flying leap off the fast track.

Ryan got his revenge later, after Cole went away. But you already know all about that.

CHAPTER 21

I rented a tan Hyundai that would have blended in anywhere people drove cars, stuck a John Deere cap on my head, wore a pair of tortoiseshell glasses with the lenses knocked out. Cole's sedan was taking up two spots in the lot outside Companion. I parked across the street and waited.

Cole came out at a little after midnight, long past closing. He'd taken to chatting with the staff while they broke the place down. What they thought of his company, I couldn't say. I'd been scarce since Cole turned up, and I had an outsider's sense that the waiters and cooks and even Max were gravitating toward him and away from me. Not that it would matter for long.

I gave Cole a half-block head start, then pulled out. Traffic was light, but I managed to keep a cab or a late-night delivery truck between us for as long as we remained downtown. I expected him to break for the highway, but he snaked his way through side streets and into the suburbs, then turned onto a broad and empty avenue. If he was looking for a tail, he'd spot me now, but at this point I didn't much care—all that mattered was that it happen away from Companion.

I reached inside my jacket, pulled my revolver from its holster, and laid it across my lap. If an opportunity came, I'd take it. A red light. A stop at a gas station. I'd have pulled up alongside him and emptied all cylinders if his windows weren't tinted. I had no interest in a fair fight. No interest in giving him his say. I wanted him gone. Afterward I'd drive to the nearest police station and confess to killing Ryan's cop. If they figured out I'd killed Cole, too, so be it.

He turned off the avenue and zigzagged his way through a complex of pastel-colored townhomes. I rolled down the passenger-side window, kept as far back as I could, one hand on the steering wheel and the other on my piece. As soon as he stepped out of his car, I'd be there. I'd call his name, wait for him to turn, fire.

But I hadn't counted on the garage with the automatic door. I cut the headlights, rolled up, watched his sedan disappear behind a slow-moving wall of off-white panels.

"Shit," I said.

I made a note of the house number, slipped my gun back in its holster, and kept driving. My chest was sore from a constant pounding. Something felt wrong. This was the kind of neighborhood Cole wouldn't wish on his worst enemy. Starter homes for working-class families. Mewling babies and gossiping housewives. Men in tank tops waxing their cars. Postage-stamp lawns and cardboard houses. Anywhere America. Which for Cole was the same as being nowhere.

I circled the block, pulled in across from Cole's unit, cut the engine, and watched. The first-floor lights were on, but I couldn't make out anyone moving behind the shades. Then the lights flicked off, and a blue television haze took their place. Cole winding down after a long night dedicated to screwing me over. I pictured him sitting in a recliner with his final scotch of the evening, his Glock on the table beside him.

The smart play would be to call it off, study his every move until I found that window when he let his guard down. But I kept seeing Ryan handcuffed to the bars of a cell while Cole's thug kicked in his ribs. I kept seeing twelve Kentucky inmates foaming at the mouth and clawing at their chests, shitting themselves and fighting for one more breath. And I knew those deaths were on me. Cole wouldn't have had a thing to lord over me if I'd been willing to put myself where Ryan was. If I'd gone straight to the nearest desk sergeant and said, *Look, it was me who killed that cop. It was drug money that bought Companion.* Let them pin Louis's murder on me, too. Truth was, if I hadn't duped him at the outset he'd still be alive. *So go ahead and lock me up,* I thought. *Because I'm hanging on by a thread as it is, and the longer I wait, the more people will get hurt.* I'd told myself I could play in deep water without drowning, but that was a lie, and there was just one way left to contain the damage, and it had to be now, tonight.

So I got out of the car and marched straight up Cole's walkway. No more hesitating. I didn't even count to three before I drew my gun and kicked the door in. Fuck it if I woke the whole neighborhood. Kids on the block would grow old talking about the night Jon Cole was murdered. Wins all around.

Except I never got a shot off. I'd pictured Cole spread out in his Barcalounger, drifting off to a rerun of *Three's Company*, but what I found was a quartet of knuckle-draggers huddled on the other side of the door, just champing to tear me apart. Cole wasn't even in the goddamned room. He waited until they had me pinned with their knees in my back and a nightstick across my neck before he made his appearance. He came strutting in from the kitchen, snapped his fingers, and said, "Let him up."

They pulled me to my feet and held my arms at my sides. Cole moved so close the toes of our shoes were touching.

"I understand the impulse," he said, "but I thought I'd trained you better than this. There's nothing more suspicious than a man in a baseball cap and a cheap rental. Still, I tried to warn you. Or didn't you wonder why it took us forty minutes to drive five miles?"

I saw now how it had played out: Cole spotting me in his rearview, picking up the phone, organizing my welcome party.

"Is this even your house?" I asked.

He stepped back, took a theatrical look at his surroundings: shag carpet, beige sectional, photos of sunsets on the walls.

"What do you think?" he asked.

I didn't answer. The leanest of the goons pointed my own gun at my temple. The others released my arms.

"Now," Cole said, "I realize you came here to kill me, but do you think we can have a civilized talk?"

I nodded. I was back to biding my time.

"Very good," he said.

He took my gun from his henchman, waved me over to the sectional. The quartet filed out of the room.

"You threw this little shindig together fast," I said.

Cole gave a modest shrug.

"You and your brother showed me just how wrong I'd been," he said. "There's no foolproof way to cultivate loyalty, and the attempt consumes gobs of time. It's all very tedious. What you want is men who ask no questions and live from one payday to the next."

"Sorry we hurt your feelings," I said.

He grinned. "Sorrier by the minute, I imagine."

We sat at opposite ends of the sectional, me leaning forward with my elbows on my knees, him sunk back, arms out to the sides like he was flanked by invisible strippers.

"I hit maximum sorry when you used me to kill twelve people," I told him.

"Oh, please," he said. "That was just a favor for a friend. I could have annihilated the entire prison and you wouldn't have come at me this way. This is about your baby brother. Even locked away, he's dragging you down. You need to forget him. Pretend he's already dead."

Something was suddenly very clear to me.

"You still believe I picked him over you," I said. "Boil away all the bullshit, and that's what this is about. Not your dead nephew. Not the missing cash. You still think you can teach me a few hard lessons and then bring me back into the fold. You can't let go. All because I was supposed to replace your prodigal kid. What was it you did to drive Roger away? I never knew. Whatever it was, it must have been bad. Something even you know is unforgivable."

That busted through the facade. He was sitting straight as an arrow now, and I could see the veins throbbing in his neck.

"You're alive because you're useful to me," he said. "You aren't in a hospital bed like your brother because I need you in front of the cameras. So I suggest you put all of your energy into remaining useful. Do you understand?"

I nodded. It didn't matter how bad I wanted to play tough guy; he was holding every card. But what bothered me most in that moment was that I couldn't make eye contact. I couldn't stop my face from going red. Like I was getting a scolding from my daddy. Like I'd broken curfew or come home with a bum report card. Like I hadn't progressed a day past the age of fourteen.

"Good. Understand this, too: Companion is mine now, in everything but name. I'm the new man behind the curtain. You work for me. The paperwork will be drafted by the end of the week. I've grown quite—"

I got to my feet. He leveled the gun at my dick.

"Sit down," he said.

He waited for me to comply, then picked up where he'd left off.

"I've grown quite fond of the place," he said. "It's classy. It has just the right amount of flare. The perfect atmosphere for business, and I have a lot of business to conduct."

"What if I refuse to sign?"

"With so many teetering dominoes, it's hard to say which one will fall. Maybe the brother domino. Maybe the dead-partner domino. Or maybe a domino I haven't yet discovered but am certain exists. You've been spending a lot of nights away from home lately. The question is, where do you sleep? And with whom?"

The best I could do was not look startled. *Bide your time*, I told myself. *Hope there's something to salvage in the end.*

"One final thing," Cole said. "Any repeat of this evening and Ryan dies. No more appeals. No more delays. And no more pretty corpse. It will be out of the judge's hands."

I stood back up, this time like I was ready to leave.

"You do that and I've got nothing more to lose," I said.

"You played that hand tonight," Cole said. "I doubt you'll be eager to try it again."

He was right about that much. I needed a new hand.

CHAPTER 22

I left Cole's feeling like I'd never sleep again if I didn't figure out how to keep my losses right where they were, because he was hell-bent on destroying everything I cared about. It didn't matter if I cared a lot or a little or somewhere in between—he wouldn't stop until the ashes were cold. If I'd had a dog, he would've poisoned it. If I'd had a boat, he would've sunk it. What Cole said to the senator all those years ago was true of me now: I was playing in his world. The best I could do was strip my life down and make the smallest possible target.

I headed straight for Companion. My brain's always been at its best when my hands are distracted and I'm forced to stand in one place, which is to say when I'm cooking. I parked out back, let myself in through the alley, switched on the bar lights, and mixed an eight-ounce kir. Looking around, it struck me that one thing hadn't changed: Companion was still a beauty. Still sleek and gleaming. How many people, I wondered, can literally stand inside the dream they built, even one time in their lives? I lifted my drink in an imaginary toast, took a long swallow, then topped it off and moved into the kitchen.

I didn't have a particular dish in mind; I just roamed the pantry and the walk-in gathering ingredients, then loaded them onto the main cutting table. Skinned chicken breasts, red and green peppers, onions, garlic, olive oil. *Keep it simple*, I thought. And I did. Easy chopping and dicing to start, followed by a slow sautéing while I spun a salad out of spinach and anchovies and feta cheese. When the chicken was cooked through, I sliced it up and spread it over the salad and dumped the whole mess in a bowl and carried the bowl back to the bar, where I lit a candle and mixed another kir.

All the while I'd been thinking.

Are you sure there's no other way? I asked myself.

But I knew the answer already. You've got to be cruel to be kind, and what could be crueler than texting your girl to say you've stopped loving her, that really you've never loved her, that you've been using her from the jump and now it was over? *Time to rip the Band-Aid right off*, I told myself. *Leave no wiggle room.* Cheryl couldn't show up on Cole's radar as anyone other than Ryan's lawyer. That meant no breakup dinner, no tearful goodbye. For once I wasn't taking any chances. Cheryl and I would never see each other again outside of a courtroom.

I typed it all into my phone: *I never loved you, I've been using you, it's over now.* For a flourish I added, *If I need to find Ryan another lawyer, so be it.* I hit "send" before my feet could go cold.

And then for a while it was like I didn't exist anymore. Like I'd gone Stepford. I ate without tasting a thing, without noticing the fork moving up and down between the bowl and my mouth. My glass emptied and filled itself.

I was rinsing my dishes when the first attack came. Somewhere between my chest and stomach, like I'd swallowed a rock or a fist and didn't know which way it would exit, only that it hurt like a son of a bitch. I ran into the bathroom and dropped my drawers and sat hunched forward on the toilet, but I'd guessed wrong—the pain was creeping north through my esophagus. I spun around, knelt with my head just above the water, and coughed up a long stream of beige bile.

I thought that would be the end of it. I flushed and stood and wiped the sweat from my forehead before a fresh wave sent me right back to my knees. The food started coming up now. Bits of pepper and chicken suspended in a throbbing web of mucus. Over and over again, until I thought there couldn't be anything left. Then I sprawled on the floor and waited for my sweat to dry.

By the time I got home I was feeling hollowed out and ready for sleep. The bright side to intense physical pain is that it clears your mind better than any meditation. For now I wasn't thinking about Cole or Ryan or twelve Kentucky inmates. I wasn't even thinking about Cheryl.

But she was thinking about me. She'd thought about me plenty while she lay there on my sofa drinking wine and smoking a joint. She was thinking so hard she didn't look up when I walked in. I forgot I'd given her a key.

"I thought maybe you'd bring the bitch back here," she said.

She swung her legs off the couch and sat up ramrod straight. She had bedhead from lying slumped against overstuffed cushions, her skin was blotchy, and the pot had turned her eyes a jagged red.

"What bitch?" I asked.

Not the brightest question, but I was feeling kind of dazed.

"Oh, I don't know," she said. "You tell me. Maxine? Ottie? One of your jailbait waitresses?"

The accusations floated right past me.

"Where did you park?" I asked.

I had visions of Cole's boys taking down plate numbers in the small visitors' lot out back.

"Don't worry," she said, "I won't ask you to walk me to my car."

"It's not that. It's just—"

"What?" she asked. "What in the hell is going on? Did you really send me that text? Was that really you who said those things? Because this feels like a shitty fucking dream."

I nodded, but if she'd asked me to say it all again out loud, I wouldn't have been able to, and she knew it.

"Why?"

There was no point in repeating a lie she hadn't believed in the first place, but the truth was too far to travel, and the best I could manage was a shrug. Cheryl didn't like that one bit.

"There's no walking that message back," she said. "I'm asking now as Ryan's lawyer. I'm here now interviewing my client's brother."

I felt like someone had turned a spotlight on me and told me to strip.

"I don't know," I said.

"You don't know?" she repeated. "What are you, twelve? Did you have a stroke? Your brother's life is at stake."

It was me sitting now and her standing, pacing the floor in front of me. She'd stubbed out her joint and shaken out her hair. She looked like herself again—sober and alert and ready to do damage.

"I don't know what you're asking me," I said.

"I'm asking you for all of it. The truth and nothing but. Everything you haven't given me so far."

"I've given you everything."

That was more than she could handle.

"My God," she shouted. "How stupid do you think I am? It was you in that apartment with Ryan. I know it was. Just like I know it was you who pulled that trigger."

I kept quiet. Her tears were like rivulets of pure rage.

"You're a fucking disaster," she said. "Give me the rest of it. Pretend I'm a priest and this is your deathbed. Every single thing you've done since you murdered that cop."

"It wasn't murder."

"What was it, then?"

"He had a gun on Ryan. He didn't identify himself. That part's true."

"Are you serious? You're going with self-defense?"

She dropped back down on the sofa.

"Start talking," she said. "Now."

It was tough going at first. My voice was all air. It felt like I was spitting words into a wind tunnel. But bit by bit it came out. Or most of it. I told her I'd bought Companion with the bag of cash

Ryan had taken off of Cole's nephew. I told her about Cole then and Cole now. I told her Louis was dead and Cole had killed him. I told her it was Cole who'd taken *Last Supper* national, though I held back the drug smuggling—maybe I'd convinced myself I wasn't sure. I told her it was Cole behind Ryan's beatings.

And then I waited while she stared at nothing like she'd wandered off into her own sad dream.

"Cheryl?" I said.

She looked up at me. Everything I wanted to say seemed either moot or absurd. How I hadn't meant to lie, not to her, but I'd fallen hard, and the things I'd kept from her were the things I'd done to survive. But then I saw Louis lying in his shallow grave and I knew that was bullshit. My sins went way beyond survival, and in any case Cheryl had quit listening. She stood and walked away almost in slow motion, and I just watched her go, thinking, *I can fix this, I can fix this, I can fix this.*

And then the door slammed shut, and I wondered if this would be the last night I ever slept in my own bed.

CHAPTER 23

But Cheryl didn't go to the cops. A week passed and no detectives came knocking. I quit scanning for SWAT but couldn't stop checking my phone every few minutes. I thought Cheryl might return my text, tell me in no uncertain terms what, upon reflection, she thought of me, and what would happen if I had the misfortune to cross her path again. But so far she'd maintained radio silence, and while she probably thought nothing more needed saying, that our relationship was dead and buried and had only ever been a sham anyway, still I allowed myself to hold out some small hope. Which was probably for the best, because otherwise I'd have been in full mourning.

And then Cole kicked the humiliation into overdrive. He had one of his knuckle-draggers dress like a lawyer and bring the paperwork to my condo. I would have thought he'd want to watch me sign, but Cole was a busy man. He was opening a rec center, giving scared-straight talks at public schools, pouring his heart out to local papers and radio stations, holding himself up as proof that rehabilitation works, all while treating Companion like his personal back room, the place where deals got hashed out and the little guy got screwed. He met with developers and contractors and inspectors and city councilmen. His idea of going legit was to make nice with anyone who could help him cut a corner, anyone he might decide to bribe later. And he introduced me to all of them as his personal chef.

Which I guess was accurate. According to the papers I'd signed, I'd officially sold my share of Companion to Cole for the sum of ten dollars, which meant he was partners with a dead man no one knew was dead. Those same papers, or maybe an addendum to those papers, demoted me to head chef and made me responsible for "daily operations" and "maintenance of the superior culinary standards already in place at Companion." Instead of incentives, Cole packed the contract full of punishment clauses. If Companion lost a star in Zagat or was dropped from a guidebook or got a bad write-up in the local gazette, my salary would take a hit. Any combination of the above and I'd be shitcanned, though we both knew that couldn't happen as long as *Last Supper* was in play.

As the pièce de résistance, he worked in a bit of language that said I'd personally cook for all special guests and parties, with the word *special* to be defined as he saw fit. If he couldn't have my love or respect, he'd damn well have me do his bidding. And it didn't take long for him to turn the burners up under my feet. The ink on our deal wasn't dry before he had me cooking quail eggs for a party of zoning commissioners and wild game for a dozen bankers interested in backing one of his schemes.

And Cole had no shortage of schemes. The problem with Cole was that he couldn't settle on a single measure of success. He wanted to be Robin Hood and the robber baron both. People had to adore him *and* he had to have more of everything than anyone else. One night he was hosting a benefit for cancer research, and the next he was wining and dining a confederacy of the Southwest's worst slumlords. The restaurant was closed for private gatherings more often than it was open, and the menu was rewritten every other night. As a business model, it was bound to fail.

Which is exactly what Cole wanted.

The truth came out quick enough. Cole brought me in on a Tuesday night to cook octopus carpaccio and Rohan duck for hedge fund types who'd traveled down from Dallas to hear his pitch for a luxury golf club he planned to build just outside Austin's city limits. There were only four potential investors, but he shuttered the restaurant anyway. Max handled the libations, and a single waiter, a college kid Cole dressed up in a vest and bow tie, ran the food out from the kitchen.

I got there hours early to prep the octopus, holding it under running water, washing away the mucus, pulling out its guts and eyes, slicing the suckers from the tentacles (this was Cole's special request). My stomach started churning almost as soon as I set foot in the kitchen. I coughed up mouthfuls of bile and drank Pepto-Bismol straight from the bottle as I went. It wasn't the fault of the octopus. The way I saw it, I'd developed an aversion. Not just to cooking but to food. Since that first bout, I'd been living on tofu and broth. If I so much as glanced at anything heavier, I could feel the acid coming on, building at the base of my chest and burning up into my esophagus. Like the thing I loved most was trying to kill me.

And still I kept telling myself, *Bide your time.*

Beyond my gut, the rest of me felt numb, like the world was still spinning but I wasn't a part of it anymore. Like people had taken a look at what I had to offer and said, *No, thanks, we'll pass.* I guess that's how it feels to have your future scripted by a sociopath. And for the first time I thought maybe I understood what Ryan was going through, pacing his cell twenty-three hours a day, knowing anything could be done to him and he couldn't do a thing in return.

When Cole's hedge fund geeks were finished with their meal, he had the waiter call me out for a bow. I took a gallows stroll to the table and just kind of shuffled in place while four anemic-looking guys in suits heaped praise on a meal I'd made from sheer muscle memory.

"Yes, indeed, gentlemen," Cole said. "James will be coming with me when I open the club. Every luxury establishment needs a star chef, and what brighter star than the host of *Last Supper*? I'm betting he'll draw a national crowd."

The geeks nearly applauded, though not one of them would admit to having seen the show. I slunk back into the kitchen, dropped my ass on a footstool, and buried my head in my hands. Cole was going to shut Companion down. That's why he ran up the overhead. That's why he turned away paying customers and threw out-of-pocket banquets. Once he opened his four-star resort, he didn't want the competition hanging around. Meanwhile, why not send me on the road, make me a minor celebrity? He was squeezing me for everything I was worth.

I felt some fight bubbling up in me then. I thought about what Cole had said that night I tailed him, about how me and Ryan proved you can't breed loyalty. He was overcorrecting now. It reminded me of a line from *The Prince*, which might be the only book I read cover to cover in twelve years of public education: *The damage you do to a man must be such that there is no chance of revenge.* Cole's kindness and Cole's meanness served the same purpose: he was keeping his subjects in line. What bothered me most was that I'd let myself be ruled. As a kid, sure, you have to be ruled by somebody, and Cole was the only one around. But now? Whatever came next, I told myself, had to be earned. Whether it was fortune or heartbreak or a quiet little life in the burbs, it had to be mine.

Meanwhile, Companion was finished. I was sitting in a graveyard, and there wasn't a thing I could do about it.

CHAPTER 24

I made a feeble stand before Cole sent me back out on the road.

"Listen," I said, "I need your word I'm not delivering another spiked batch. Kill me and Ryan both if you have to—I'm not a mass murderer."

We were sitting at the bar just after Companion closed for the night. Instead of answering, he said, "You've lost weight. A lot of weight."

It was true. I could barely keep my pants up with my belt buckled through the last hole. Sometimes I felt weak. Sometimes I thought that if I put my mind to it, I could float away. I didn't press the conversation any further. Chances are I'd have made the delivery one way or the other.

Last Supper headed to Alabama. I ghost-walked my way through every leg of the trip, got to the hotel at a little after midnight, and dropped face forward onto the bed with my clothes on and my shoes on and the lights on, and I didn't move a muscle until the wake-up call came at 5:00 a.m. After a breakfast of toast and hot water, I got in the car and went where the GPS sent me. Cole had found yet another backwoods mechanic, and this time the trailer had a TV and an antenna that picked up three Birmingham stations. I watched *Good*

Day Alabama until the long-short beeps signaled the all clear, and then it was on to the prison.

I drove back and forth through the gates without Bill having to tell me; I just kept going until he said stop. I coasted through the episode like it was a fill-in-the-blank eulogy. *We are gathered here today to mourn the passing of* X. The inmate was an X. The cooking was an X. The meal was an X. I was just completing the form so I could go home. The only bright spot was that Timmy had been caught snorting coke in a Taco Bell bathroom and landed himself in a Florida rehab resort.

When I deplaned in Austin and switched on my phone, I found an hour-old text message from Cheryl. Seeing her name there in my hand made my body stall out. I stood on the causeway with people breaking around me, my thumb hovering for a long beat before I slid the message open. All it said was, *I have something for you. Come pick it up.*

The flight had been bumpy as hell and my gut was aching, though I hadn't eaten more than a handful of fish crackers since breakfast. I bought a ginger ale from a vending machine, took slow sips all the way to Cheryl's place while I tried to believe she might have forgiven me. The odds were long: I'd killed a cop and used the cash from a crime my brother committed to start a business. That wasn't ace behavior, but in my defense I did think I was saving Ryan's life, and there'd been no one to give the money back to. Cheryl knew I came from nothing. I was exactly the kind of person she'd set out to champion, and I guess that was what attracted her to me: I'd risen above my station and done it on my own terms. Or so she'd thought.

By the time I rang her bell, I gave myself a fifty-fifty shot: 50 percent she wanted me back; 50 percent it'd be the cops who answered. The door swung right open, and it was Cheryl on the other side, looking like she'd been standing there waiting, like maybe this was something she wanted to get over with before her courage ran out.

"Jesus," she said, giving me a once-over. "What the hell happened to you?"

"What do you mean?"

"It's like you left a third of yourself someplace else."

"Stomach virus," I said. "I'm back on solid food now."

She stood for a minute, framed by the doorway, silhouetted by the apartment light. She was wearing jeans, a baggy men's tee, nothing on her feet, little to no makeup. Her hair was pulled back in a ponytail with a few strands hanging wild. Like she hadn't been expecting anyone in the world.

"Come in," she said. "I don't want the neighbors to hear this."

And then we were huddled toe-to-toe in her narrow foyer, neither of us saying a word until I blurted out, "I really miss you."

It was true. No matter what I did or thought about, missing her was always there.

"And I miss who I thought you were," she said.

Her voice wasn't angry or sad, cold or cruel. It wasn't anything at all. I followed her into the dining room. She took a crumpled paper bag off the table and handed it to me. It weighed about as much as a roll of pennies.

"I don't know what's inside," she said. "Or where it came from, or what you should do with it. And don't open it here."

Another stab at plausible deniability.

"What about Ryan?" I asked.

"What about him?"

"His case, I mean. Should we—"

"I work for your brother," she said. "If he wants to update you, he will."

There was nothing more to say. I thanked her for whatever was in the bag and turned to leave, but something dead center in my torso refused to turn with me. I felt like one of those action figures from the eighties with the elastic bands running through their bodies so they could twist and pivot and bend at the waist. My band snapped. It shot up and struck me in the gut. I stopped in my tracks, braced myself with one hand against the wall.

And then it came gushing out. Sixteen ounces of ginger ale mixed with bile and bits of fish cracker, all over Cheryl's shiny hardwood floor. The explosion ended with me on my knees, panting and mumbling, "Jesus Christ, I'm so sorry."

She touched my back, and I heard her giggling softly, or trying not to giggle in that nervous way that says, *Well, here we are.*

"Are you okay?" she asked. "Is it over? Do you need the bathroom?"

"No," I said. "I'm done."

"You sure?"

"Yeah. Just let me catch my breath. I'll clean this up and go."

"I doubt you could clean up a drop of water right now," she said.

She helped me to my feet, led me to the couch, then came back with a damp washcloth. I was light-headed. I couldn't stop sweating.

"Just hold this to your forehead and shut your eyes for a minute," she instructed.

"Thank you," I said.

She left to deal with my mess, and for a brief moment I could hear her giggling again. When she'd finished wiping and mopping and sanitizing, she came and sat with me.

"That's new," she said. "Does it happen often?"

I nodded, held my eyes shut. This was all wrong. It was always supposed to be me taking care of her.

"It just started out of the blue," I told her. "I don't know what's going on."

"It's like your body gave acid reflux the key to the city," she said. "You need to get it checked out. Unless you want stomach cancer."

And though she'd been nursing me with a damn gentle touch, still I didn't hear a hint of warmth in her voice.

•

Outside, I sat in my car for a long while, looking up at Cheryl's window, willing her to stick her head out and call me back. I waited like I had nowhere else in the world to be.

The lights in her apartment switched off.

I opened the bag. Inside, I found what looked like three button cell batteries, one larger battery, and a flash drive. I shook them down into the palm of my hand, thinking, *What the hell?*

And then I understood. Not batteries, but listening devices and a GPS tracker. I looked back up at Cheryl's window and smiled. I knew exactly what I was supposed to do.

CHAPTER 25

Instructions on the flash drive told me to conceal the devices in the kinds of places I'd never dusted or even thought to look for dust. I stuck the first bug under Cole's habitual table at Companion, the second under the dashboard of his car, just below the steering wheel. He drove an old-model Jaguar, old enough to break into with a coat hanger. I hid the tracking device under the wheel well. The third bug I shoved down into the lining of a leather jacket he hardly ever wore but carried with him everywhere. I had a brief worry that he might sweep the car, but it was early for that. His enterprise, legit or not, wasn't fully up and running. There was no reason for anyone to be looking at him. At least not that closely.

Meanwhile, Cole tethered me to the shortest leash he could find. He fired Maxine and refused to replace her, said he'd hire a temp when I was off shooting *Last Supper*. It was his way of keeping me where he could find me, anchored to the kitchen morning through night. When Max quit in solidarity with his sister, Cole had a new barkeep waiting in the wings: Garrett, an ageless, six-foot-seven bruiser who shaved his head to the bone and wore dark shirts that reflected the bar's track lighting. It wasn't hard to imagine he came with a second skill set.

Nights, I'd get home feeling exhausted, eat a banana and a sleeve of saltines, then curl up in bed with my laptop and start listening to the day's recordings. It would have been a cure for insomnia if it wasn't for the off chance that something big was just around the bend. At first, information came slow, or not at all. The car produced little I could use, since he was barely in it except for short rides to and from Companion. His lunches and dinners with business types didn't reveal much beyond what I already knew: he was opening a country club, claimed it had always been his dream, joked that he could only get into one if his name was hanging on the sign.

Of course, I didn't really know what I was listening for. I had no idea what an Achilles' heel would sound like—only that it had to be loud, and it couldn't lead back to me or Ryan. In general, Cole was chattier than I'd ever realized. He talked his way from one end of the day to the other, and when he was alone, he sang: Sinatra and Martin and Bennett—crooners he must have grown up listening to. And the fucker could carry a tune. I wondered why I'd never heard him before, but of course I knew: singing was a bit of softness he kept to himself.

Cole was damn good at talking, too. He could play nice and make you fall for him, or he could play mean and make you damn glad he was talking to someone else. Like all the best politicians, he bounced from one mood to the next in the time it took to dial a fresh number. He could sweet-talk a zoning commissioner and ream out a contractor without so much as a sip of water in between. Cole had talent. Talent, but no cause. At least not a real one. He was restless. He set things in motion the way other people breathe. But in the end that's all it was: motion. Cole was a kite in a tempest. I'd just have to wait for the wind to die down.

Three weeks in, I got a bite. An early morning call that sounded promising, though I could only hear Cole's side of the conversation.

"I thought you were only going to contact me if there was an update," he said. "Telling me there's nothing new isn't an update. If you charged by the result instead of the hour, you'd be on welfare instead of my tit."

He could have been talking about anything—a stock price or a building permit or a ticket to a sold-out prizefight—but I recognized the strained edge in his voice: it surfaced whenever something personal bled into his business. Something important to him. Something he had to correct or set right before he could take one more step. I only hoped that whoever he'd been talking to would call again.

Meanwhile, Cole continued the campaign to clean up his image. He found another local TV station to profile him. The piece started with a cold open on one of his scared-straight talks. The camera spent a long beat on Cole's face while he told a story about showering in prison, then panned back to reveal a gymnasium full of riveted middle schoolers. The cynic in me wondered if there was trick editing involved, like maybe they'd shown the kids a horror film and then spliced in their reactions with Cole's jabber.

From the gymnasium, the profile jumped to the groundbreaking ceremony for Cole's new rec center. He stood outside on a clear day, wearing a pale-blue suit and a ridiculous neon hard hat. People fawned all around him while he played humble. He kept his remarks short, focused on *the kids*. The sound of jackhammers broke up a long round of applause.

Then it was on to Companion, where I made a reluctant cameo. This time I had to play nice. Cole held me up as a model of what a good rec center can do for a child. I felt like a dog who'd learned all his master's favorite tricks. He made it sound like we hadn't been out of touch a day in the last twenty years. He talked about all the great things we were going to do together. When the interviewer pressed him, he winked and said details would be forthcoming.

End of profile.

Back in the real world, cooking had become a full-on battle. Just being around food was enough to trigger an attack, and I couldn't knead dough or gut a fish or so much as chop parsley without downing a handful of ranitidine tablets first. It felt to me like I'd reached the end of something—the something that mattered—and was just waiting for an announcement to make it official. Like I was floating through the days on my own death-raft. Memories I hadn't touched in forever surfaced when I stood at the stove. I'd flash on the babysitter, a kid herself, putting down the phone and turning to me and Ryan with a lost-in-the-woods look, and I remembered knowing before she said a word: they were dead. I'd see Aunt Joan, one of the rare times she decided to play parent, waking up drunk and stoned, threatening to walk us to school, then passing out again with her face in a bowl of Apple Jacks. I was beginning to understand why Ryan wanted out. Maybe beyond a certain point there's no such thing as healing. Maybe you just run yourself ragged pretending.

CHAPTER 26

But then I learned some more about the failed update, and everything changed. Cole took the call in his car, in the middle of the day, when I knew he was at Companion. He must have stepped out for privacy, which meant whatever he wanted to discuss didn't fit with his new facade.

"Yes, I received the photos," he said. "That's all well and good, but if you had him in your sights, then why don't you know where he is now? . . . Then why didn't you buy a ticket? . . . No, don't. I'll drive down there myself. We're overdue for a chat anyway."

The next morning he called the restaurant to say something had come up and he'd be heading out on an overnight trip. Why he bothered calling in, I don't know: it's not like he had anything to do with day-to-day operations. I hired Maxine back for a short off-the-books tour, then sped home.

I figured I'd listen in live, make a party of it. I got back into my pajamas, brewed a pot of weak tea, propped the pillows against my headboard, and fired up my laptop. I opened three tabs: one for the bug in his car, one for the bug in his jacket, and one for the GPS. When everything was set up the way I liked, I sat back and waited.

The GPS showed his car heading west on I-84. The trip started out with Cole singing Johnny Cash's *At Folsom Prison*—the entire album, track by track. Then there was nothing but a low hum for a long while. I tried to think of where he might be going, but didn't have the slightest notion. Maybe he'd jump off at Lubbock or continue all the way up to Vegas. Maybe he was aiming for the Pacific Ocean. You couldn't be sure of a quick trip with Cole because flying was the one thing he'd admit terrified him.

I drifted off for a while, then got up and carried the laptop into the kitchen and set it on the counter while I reheated a bowl of noodle soup. When I was done eating, I carried the computer back to bed. Nothing had changed. Cole was still chugging along I-84. An hour later he pulled over at a rest stop, filled the tank, and went inside. For once he didn't take the leather jacket with him, and I thought maybe this was it and I'd have no way of knowing. But just ten minutes later he was back on the road, still heading west.

After a full day of driving, he exited the highway at Albuquerque. I figured he was looking for a place to spend the night, but the GPS tracked him to the far side of town, then showed him turning in circles like he was lost. The car came to a stop halfway down a dead-end street.

It was late now, well past dark, and Cole was wearing his jacket in the cool night air. I heard what sounded like someone leaning on a doorbell, followed by a fist banging against hollow wood. When the banging stopped, it was Cole who spoke first.

"You'd point a gun at your benefactor?" he said.

"I'd point a gun at anyone who came unannounced at this hour."

All I could tell about the voice was that it belonged to a man much older than Cole.

"Aren't you going to invite me in?"

"I got a choice?"

"I've driven all this way."

"That's what worries me."

"Relax. I never deliver bad news myself."

The old man relented. I heard weight moving on worn floorboards, and then a news anchor went quiet.

"Guess I should ask if you want something to drink."

"Don't bother. This isn't a social call."

"What kind of call is it?"

"You know why I'm here. Where is he?"

"Who?"

"He doesn't live with you now, does he?"

"Roger? That boy has no use for me."

"Then why was he here?"

Neither of them said anything for a while. I started to form an image of the old man. Frail body, baggy T-shirt, pants buckled just under his chest. A man withering away. A man without a purpose. Cole would give him equal billing with a dust mite.

"How'd you know about that?" the old man asked, his voice a pitch higher and a touch weaker now.

"How did you think you could keep it from me?" Cole said.

"I didn't keep a thing from you. He popped up, and then he was gone. I wasn't waiting on him any more than I was waiting on you."

"Bullshit. If he isn't here, then you must have a number for him."

"He looked me up. That's all I know."

"That's all you know? I want my son."

"And I want Kenny. I want my grandson."

"I had nothing to do with that. I was locked away."

"Who put him on the street in the first place?"

"It's not like you've been turning down my money."

"That's hush money, and we both know it. I got stories you don't want told."

"I wouldn't be reminding me of that just now. Where's my son?"

"I never said nothing to Roger. And I got no idea where he is."

"But he came to see you."

"He was in town. That's all."

"To visit you? I guess that makes sense. I guess I'm what the two of you have in common. You must have had some fun at my expense."

"It wasn't like that."

"What name is he going by now?"

"I just called him Roger."

"Are you sure? I found out he was here. I'll find out if you're lying."

"I ain't lying."

They went quiet again, and I thought for sure it would turn violent now. I pictured Cole with the old man's throat in his hands, tightening and relaxing, tightening and relaxing. I picked up the phone, was about to call Albuquerque PD when I heard first one door slam, then another. Cole was back in his car.

I must have been breathing as hard as the old man.

To hell with my gut, I thought, and poured myself a scotch.

Little by little, it all started to fit together. The old man was Cole's father-in-law. Grandfather to Roger and Kenny, the nephew Ryan robbed and killed. Cole had hired a PI to find his son.

And there it was: Roger, the Achilles' heel.

I had a place to start, but I needed more information. I needed to hear those stories Cole didn't want told.

CHAPTER 27

He camped at a hotel off the highway. I didn't hesitate. I got dressed, fished the last of Ryan's robbery money out of a false vent above the stove, packed my laptop and some clothes into a day bag, and hit the road. I'd be in Albuquerque by ten the next morning. Maybe I'd pass Cole on the interstate. Chances were he'd stop at a casino on the way home. With any luck, I'd be back before he knew I was gone.

I swallowed three ranitidine tablets, slid a hard rock mix Ryan made for my sixteenth birthday into the stereo, spun the volume to max once I hit the highway. Austin to Albuquerque is a lot of miles to spend thinking. Mostly my mind circled the same question: how would I get the old man to talk to me? Kenny's family had steered clear of Ryan's trial, but what if the old man recognized me from *Last Supper*? Would that be a good thing or a bad thing? Bad if he knew the backstory—if he knew it was my brother who killed his boy.

By the time I hit the New Mexico border, the sun was rising behind me, lighting up the desert. I'd lived a day's drive away my whole life but had never been here before. I didn't know that rock and scrub could make so many colors. I spotted a herd of antelope, swerved to miss a turkey vulture feasting on a flattened armadillo. I stopped for gas in a town where even the McDonald's was an adobe.

My brain was shaking with sleeplessness, but I was sharp enough to realize that Cole might be planning another visit to the old man's place. I reached the outskirts of Albuquerque, found a diner that offered free Wi-Fi, ordered a plate of flapjacks, and checked Cole's tracker. He was on his way home, about a hundred miles into his drive. No chance of him walking in on me and his father-in-law.

The old man's house both was and wasn't what I'd expected. Somehow I knew it would be small and squat and sided with linoleum. The faded green trim didn't surprise me, and neither did the small awning covering the concrete slab that passed for a porch. What caught me off guard was the garden, a small but carefully sculpted maze of thriving cacti and lavender and other shrubs and flowers I couldn't name. I'd imagined a man broken by the loss of his daughter and grandson, gnarled and guilt-ridden, not facing the day so much as waiting it out. But here was a garden that required daily care, and whether he tended to it himself or not, it said something about how he lived. It said he hadn't quit.

I sat parked at the curb, still not sure how I'd get him to open his door or how I'd explain myself once he did. It wasn't that we lacked common ground—we were bookend testaments to how many lives a single man could turn upside down—but on my side that common ground led straight to Ryan, and Ryan wasn't going to win me any favors.

I decided to wing it. Ring the bell and see what I came up with when the door opened. I reached behind me, pulled the paper sack filled with cash from the back seat, set my phone to record, and started up the stone path.

It was a long time before he answered. Long enough for my mind to start running scenarios. Maybe Cole spooked him worse than I'd imagined. Maybe he'd swallowed a sedative too many and was lying unconscious in a back room. Maybe he'd had a heart attack. Or maybe the hangover from Cole's surprise appearance had just made him shy about unannounced visits.

I was about to press the button again when I heard a chain slide free of its latch, and then I was staring through the mesh screen at a man who wasn't the withered and broken octogenarian I'd pictured, but rather a six-foot-plus, bare-chested brute who looked like he could still bench my weight on his worst day.

"Yeah?" he said.

"I'm a friend of Roger's," I told him.

I don't know why I said it. There were a hundred ways he might know I was lying. For all I knew, he'd been lying to Cole, and Roger was tucked away somewhere in the far reaches of the house.

"From way back," I added. "I'm not sure he'd even remember me."

Which was equally dumb, because if Roger and I weren't in touch, how would I know where to find his grandfather?

"I got a forty-five tucked in the back of my jeans," the man said, "and I've lived too long to believe in coincidence. So why don't you just tell me what it is you've got to do with that piece of shit who came to see me last night."

The good news: he showed no sign of recognizing me.

"Fair enough," I said. "You and I have an enemy in common."

"Well, the enemy of my enemy might be my friend, or he might just be another douchebag," the old man said. "I don't know you, and I got no reason to trust you, so I'm gonna call this meeting closed."

He started to shut the door.

"Wait," I said.

Without any explanation, I opened the sack and held it up so he could see inside.

"What's that for?" he asked.

"I want to know why Cole's been paying you," I said. "If you tell me—depending on the reason—he may not be paying you much longer. That's what this money is for. So you have no more motive to keep quiet."

His eyes slid up and down between me and the bag.

"How do I know this ain't a trap? How do I know it ain't Cole himself who sent you?"

I pointed to a wrought iron bench in the garden.

"Let's talk," I said. "Outside, in full daylight."

He thought it over.

"Okay," he said. "But the forty-five comes with me."

•

The yard was so dense with flowers that I had to tuck my feet far under the bench.

"That money's for me, huh?" he asked.

I nodded.

"Provided I give you the answer you want."

He took a deep breath, ran a hand over his stubble. I adjusted the phone in my pocket.

"All right," he said. "How much do you know already?"

"I know Roger's your grandson. I know he came to see you."

"You know about Kathy?"

"His mother?"

"My daughter."

"I know Roger blames Cole for her death."

"Roger doesn't know the half. Cole pays me to keep it that way. I tell you, and like you said, he won't be paying me any longer. Hell, he'll kill me if he can."

I picked up the bag, gave it a light shake.

"Yeah, right," he said. "Thing is, I swore I'd never tell anyone. For my own damn sake. But I guess secrets are the only thing I got left to give."

He looked at me like he was wondering for the first time who I might be.

"That prick must have done something to you," he said.

I nodded.

"No surprise. He's done something to everyone he's ever met. Maybe he's got some horror show in his past that explains it all, or maybe he's just evil."

He paused, seemed to be gearing up for the big reveal.

"Here's the long and the short of it," he said. "Kathy got addicted to the shit he was selling. She OD'd. On purpose. Cole lost his mind. He set the fire to cover it up. He had so many damn enemies, no one doubted it was arson. That's what Roger always thought—it was somebody after his father who killed his mother. He happened to be staying with me and his grandma at the time. He and Kenny both."

"How do you know this?" I asked.

"Kathy said goodbye. In a letter. It was addressed to me and her mother, but I was the one who read it."

"You still have it?"

"Destroyed it before I got to the last word. And yeah, I went along with Cole's lie. I didn't want her mother to know. I didn't want Roger to know."

"But you told Cole you knew?"

"I went straight at the motherfucker. I didn't have proof, but Kathy gave too much detail for him to doubt me. If he'd been in his right mind, he might have thought to say she was freebasing, set that fire herself. But the way he was, I think he wanted me to kill him. And if I'd had it in me, that's what I'd have done."

"And he's been paying you ever since?"

"I didn't ask for it. He was terrified Roger'd find out. I know it sounds like I made out off my girl's death, and I ain't proud of it. But I wasn't going to the cops anyway. Too many people would've been hurt by it. Kathy's memory would've been hurt. And Cole didn't kill her. Not the quick death that came at the end."

"How do I get in touch with Roger?"

"So you can tell him? Turn him against his old man? More than he's turned already, that is."

"Roger's an adult now."

He wavered. I set the bag on his lap.

"Listen," I said. "Cole's a cancer. He plays saint, and that confuses people long enough for him to settle in and start tearing them apart. Not just people, but families. Communities. The worst kind of evil knows how to disguise itself, and that's Cole. He made your daughter love him, and then he made her an addict. He took me under his wing after my parents died. He told me I had talent, and he helped me develop that talent. He made me feel like somebody. And then when I was old enough to be useful, he started reminding me just how much I owed him. I was a teenage boy with no people to speak of, and he turned me into a street thug. I'd give my life to take back some of the things I did for him. You know what I'm talking about. He did the same to Kenny. And he's not finished. Back in Austin, he's started recruiting. He's giving talks at schools and opening a new rec center. If the people he's hurt already, the living ones, don't keep him from ruining more lives, then who will? I know it seems like nothing sticks to Cole. I know sometimes he seems invincible, but he's not. He's flesh and blood, and flesh and blood can be stopped. A man can wake up king of the world and go to bed a slave if the right people turn against him."

"You mean his son?"

"And you. And me."

He dropped his head, then raised it again.

"Roger's got an email address," he said. "Gave me a little computer so I could write him. Of course, I can barely figure how to turn the thing on."

He got up, left the bag on his chair, and walked into the house. I heard the door lock behind him, and after a minute I wondered if he was coming back. But then the lock spun again, and he stepped out and handed me a piece of paper.

"And you can keep this," he said, taking up the bag and shoving it at my chest. "I've been making money off that man's misery for too long."

"You might want to do some traveling," I told him.

"Nah," he said, patting his .45. "I'm too damn old for new scenery."

CHAPTER 28

I'd have driven straight back to Austin if I could have made it on a single tank of gas. By the time I got home, I'd been up forty-eight hours, but I wasn't ready for bed yet. I sprawled out on the living room floor, fired up the laptop, and checked in on Cole. Like I'd suspected, he'd taken a detour before crossing the state line, spent the night at a reservation casino. Bad news always sent Cole to the blackjack table. He wouldn't be home for a while yet.

I downloaded the recording I'd made in Albuquerque, listened to be sure it was clear, then opened a new email account with a fake name I hoped would sound legit. In the subject line, I typed, *A message from your grandfather.* I left the body blank. If Roger wanted to find Cole, he'd know how to do it. I hit "send," then slept straight through the night for the first time in forever.

•

A week went by and nothing happened. Cole was still a daily presence at Companion. If anything was bothering him, he put on a brave face. Roger hadn't answered my email, but then I didn't really expect him to. Either he'd make a move or he wouldn't. Meanwhile, I was stuck in that limbo between waiting and giving up.

The next episode of *Last Supper* brought me back to Huntsville. I stopped at the same mechanic's shop on the way, bought breakfast from the same street vendor. Timmy was absent again, serving out a prolonged stint in his rehab-resort rather than face possession charges. Bill seemed to have given up on the notion that *Last Supper* was his chance to reform the penal system through documentary art. I saw it in him right away. He looked kind of browbeaten and sad. Maybe news of his producer's powder habit made him realize he was looking for fame and social justice in the wrong place. Personally, I didn't mind him phoning it in. For once we nailed my entrance in a single take.

Jimmy Bernhard, the subject of the episode, lived in the cell next to Ryan's. He was the only inmate I'd heard Ryan mention by name. Ryan liked the guy. They talked to each other through an air duct, and I knew most of Jimmy's story before I sat down to interview him. He'd been convicted in the shooting deaths of his two daughters, ages eleven and thirteen. He claimed he was innocent, and Ryan believed him. Ryan believed him because in two years his story never changed. According to Jimmy, his older brother had called earlier that night in a state beyond despair. He'd been laid off the week before, and his girlfriend had left him that morning. He sounded intoxicated and was threatening to swallow a bottle of barbiturates. Jimmy hopped in the car and drove straight to Dallas. But when he got there, the brother was nowhere to be found. By the time he made it back home, his daughters were dead, killed with the handgun he kept in his nightstand.

The police questioned the brother, who admitted to calling but denied having talked about anything more urgent than arrangements for an upcoming camping trip. Jimmy couldn't offer any better motive than a psychotic break, which the detectives assigned to the case clearly didn't buy. So Jimmy went to jail, then death row. That was sixteen years ago.

He wouldn't say a word while we set up in his cell. Then he refused to look at me or the cameras.

"Are you scared?" I asked.

"I'm innocent," he said, his eyes pointed at the wall behind me.

"Tell me about that," I said. "How did you wind up here?"

"I'm innocent," he repeated. "Killing me is a crime. Who will put the state to death?"

"I'm here to talk about your final meal," I said.

He ignored me, started again from the top: "I'm innocent. Killing me is a crime. Who will put the state to death?"

"I'm not here to talk about the state," I said.

But he recited the same three phrases again.

Bill called for a break. He tried to reason with Jimmy. When that didn't work, he pleaded.

"If I accept a last meal," Jimmy said, "it means I accept the state's punishment. I don't. The state owes me my life, not a dinner. They call it prosecution. I call it persecution."

"But why deny yourself one last luxury?" Bill asked.

"They call it prosecution. I call it persecution," Jimmy repeated, this time louder and with a singsong intonation.

"But we have the very best—"

"They call it prosecution. I call it persecution. Who will put the state to death?"

It was a chant now. Other inmates joined in, up and down the block. Bill signaled for the cameras to start filming, maybe with an eye to the special features DVD. The voices swelled. The building seemed to sway. When the guards couldn't restore quiet, they ushered us out. There was nothing more to do. I couldn't cook air. Jimmy had won a small victory on his last day.

Ryan was still in the infirmary but out of critical care and well enough for us to keep our visit. Since my workday was cut short, Ottie authorized my early entry to the conjugal apartment. The CO asked if he should bring Ryan over straightaway, and I said, "No, let's stick to the schedule." I took a long nap and followed it up with a scalding shower. Then I swallowed a half dozen ranitidine tablets, plus the probiotics I'd added to the mix. The menu for the evening featured corned brisket and candied yams, another store-bought dish. Just heating it up brought acid to the back of my throat.

Ryan's bruises had faded, and his spirits had changed for the better. He looked . . . not happy, but like happiness was no longer out of the question.

"Did she tell you?" he asked.

We were back at the dining room table, and I was wishing like hell that we could share a drink.

"Did who tell me what?"

"Cheryl got me an appeal. A new judge is gonna hear my case. They set a date and everything. It's a few months off, but still."

I felt a pang at the mention of Cheryl's name. Then it sunk in.

"Jesus Christ, Ryan," I said. "That's the best fucking news I've ever heard."

And it was. It felt real—like something real would come of it. When Cheryl got wind of an opportunity, she could work miracles. I thought of Jimmy Bernhard and wished he had a Cheryl in his corner. Most likely he'd been assigned a public defender who was working a dozen other cases out of a soggy office in a municipal basement.

"You sure about that?" Ryan asked. "You seem kind of glum. And thin as fuck."

"But not as thin as you."

"Hey, I put on weight. Food's good in the infirmary. And there are lots of eyes. No way for a CO to come at me."

He stiffened for a beat, and I knew what he was thinking.

"You'll be in gen pop soon enough," I said.

I watched him eat and let myself imagine that Cheryl was with us, that we were all together in a real living room with music in the background and champagne in our glasses. In another life, we'd have made a damn fine family.

CHAPTER 29

The nurse switched on some flute-heavy classical music that sounded to me like an anxious fat man trying to whistle, then jammed a needle in my arm and emptied the syringe.

"Now, you just lie down and think nice thoughts," she said.

By the time the doctor showed up, I was sort of conscious and sort of not. I must have stayed that way, because all through the procedure I could hear the flute playing but I couldn't feel what he was doing inside me; couldn't feel the tube wending its way through my esophagus, pushing past the bile and mucus to find whatever it was that had me doubled over in the bathroom if I ate so much as a slice of toast.

An hour later I was woozy as hell but awake and back in my own clothes. The doctor opened the door and stuck his head in. He talked fast and didn't bother to lift his mask.

"It's simple," he said. "You've got GERD."

"GERD?"

"Gastroesophageal reflux disease. It's essentially chronic indigestion with some nasty side effects. Your stomach is kicking food and acid back up into your esophagus."

Maybe it was the drug residue, but I damn near burst into tears.

"Chronic?" I said. "I'm a chef. What am I supposed to do?"

He shrugged.

"I'll write you a script for Prilosec. It's cheaper that way. Just be sure to avoid fatty foods. If that doesn't work, you might try cognitive therapy. Stress is a common trigger."

And then it was off to the next patient while I imagined plunking down on a shrink's couch and launching into my confession. The confidentiality clause would have to be airtight.

I left the doctor's office at a little before noon and started walking. I could have gone straight home—I only lived a few blocks away—but even though I was hungry from fasting and groggy from the sedative, home was the last place I wanted to be. I kept going right past my door and into the heart of downtown.

Hedge fund types were creeping out for their lunches now. I looked around at the chain stores and retail shops and the smokers standing on corners and in front of buildings, and I thought, *I'm only here because I never left*. I thought about Ryan and Cole and Cheryl, about Huntsville and Companion, and I told myself I could have gotten into the same mess anywhere, that life is life wherever you live it. But deep down that didn't feel the least bit true.

It's that doctor, I told myself.

He'd left me feeling that nothing would get better, that every ray of hope would die with a shrug and a placebo.

But there was more to it than that. Austin was a fine city, but I wanted to be someplace where no one remembered what I looked like when I was twelve. Someplace where I could fall down and not have a soul but myself to blame for it. Someplace where the world would look just a little unfamiliar every time I stepped outside.

But for now that was all just fantasy aimed at nowhere in particular. I couldn't run until I knew exactly what I'd be leaving behind, and how much of it was likely to come chasing after me.

●

It happened later that night, just shy of closing. I was standing at Cole's table. I'd eaten nothing but bone broth and Prilosec all day. Cole was courting a golf pro he hoped would sponsor a grand-opening tournament at his resort. The guy was pushing fifty, with a bow-shaped upper spine and a fluffy midsection, but as he said himself, golf isn't exactly the decathlon. He'd ordered a fish stew and wanted to know what kind of stock I used.

"Clam juice," I told him. "It's simplest and best."

"Interesting," he said. "And I guess in theory you could make it with any assortment of fish?"

"Cod and halibut work best," I said. "You need a nice, firm white fish. Scallops and shrimp work, too, but I'd stay away from anything too delicate or oily. I tried tuna once and had to throw the batch away."

I thought I caught Cole's eyes rolling back with boredom and was about to excuse myself when he reached out and grabbed my forearm. I looked down, saw he'd broken out in a fast sweat.

"You all right?" I asked.

He just pointed. I turned, saw the spitting image of the Cole I first met at Austin Rec: same close-cropped brown hair, same stocky frame, same beaked nose and low-rise neck. He stood at the center of the restaurant, pulling at a thread on the double-breasted peacoat he had no business wearing in eighty-degree weather, his eyes darting around like he couldn't make them rest on any one object.

"My son," Cole whispered.

He started to rise. Roger spotted him, reached into his coat, and pulled out a long-barreled revolver.

"Down, down, down!" Garrett shouted from behind the bar.

Roger pivoted, fired in Garrett's direction. There was an explosion of glass and alcohol. Patrons screamed, ran, dropped to the floor. Garrett ducked down, came back up holding a Glock 9. He fired, missed, blew out the plate glass window fronting the street. Roger brandished a chair like it was some kind of shield, started moving toward Cole while firing over his shoulder. Garrett crouched, steadied his arm against the bar, squeezed off two more rounds. The first hit Roger in the knee; the second brought him down.

Cole screamed until he was out of air. Then everything went quiet, or maybe the whirling in my ears drowned out every other sound. I scrambled to my knees on the floor. I didn't see that Cole had his piece out. Neither did Garrett. Cole dropped him with a single shot, then crossed to the bar, leaned over, and emptied his clip. The last of the patrons and staff filed through the missing window. It was just me and Cole and as many sirens bearing down as I've ever heard at one time. Cole looked over at Roger's body.

"He didn't say a word," he told me. "He didn't say why."

Then Cole dropped his gun and fled.

•

I spent most of the following week getting grilled by detectives and FBI agents who didn't like seeing an informant they'd pardoned turn repeat offender. It seemed like anyone I talked to knew everything about me. They knew how and when Cole and I met. They knew Ryan killed Cole's nephew. They knew Cole bought my share of Companion for nothing. They took what they knew and went on to assume a whole lot. Namely, they assumed Cole and I were partners in more than a restaurant.

Companion was shuttered, in tatters, a crime scene. There was no future in it for me. No one would risk taking their family out to eat in a combat zone, which is what the local papers were calling it now. Besides, Companion belonged to Cole, and Cole was a fugitive. The state would seize it once they realized Louis was missing.

The media wasted no time grinding me into dust. The general theme was that where there's smoke there's fire. In my case, the smoke included Ryan and Cole and *Last Supper*. Anyone who spent so much of his life around criminals had to be one himself. The more generous opinion pieces called me a soul damaged beyond all hope of mending; others called me a menace and a thug and argued that since I was bound to end up in prison anyway, they might as well lock me up now.

My television career was over and done, too. I wasn't in a position to put a friendly face on anyone's death camp. Whether they'd replace me or scrap the show altogether remained to be seen. Under any other circumstances, I would have felt relieved.

Meanwhile, the listening devices had gone silent. Cole was in the wind, and I had a hell of a time convincing law enforcement that

I didn't know where he'd gone. Austin Homicide kept me in their box for eighteen straight hours. Their resident good cop must have been out sick, because I was tag-teamed by two dough-shaped sadists who never appeared in the room at the same time and always repeated each other's questions. In between, they cracked a lot of jokes about what I'd cook for Cole in his final hours. At around five in the morning, my resolve gave out.

"Listen," I told the bald one, "this routine is getting tired."

"What routine is that?"

"The one where you and your partner try to catch me in a lie. If you even have a partner. If that isn't just you in a fake mustache and a toupee."

"Watch your mouth, kid."

"I'm not a kid. You brought me in as a witness and now you're treating me like a suspect."

I looked up at the camera.

"They haven't read me a single right," I said. "I want that on the record."

He must have sensed the *L* word coming.

"Easy now," he said. "No one said you're a suspect. But as far as we can tell, you know the guy better than anyone. He went on TV and called you his son."

"Yeah, well, you saw how well he gets along with his sons. Our arrangement was strictly business. He wanted to move Companion to the resort he was building. He convinced me there was money in it. Check the paperwork if you don't believe me."

"We'd check it even if we did believe you."

"Fair enough," I said. I stood up. "I've done my best to cooperate. Unless you want to charge me, I'm going to bed. I won't leave town, I'll call if I hear anything, et cetera, et cetera. I know you don't believe me, but no one wants to see Cole rot in a cage more than I do."

He smiled, took a step back, and held the door open for me. I left wishing Roger hadn't been such an amateur.

CHAPTER 30

A month passed and still no Cole. I put my condo on the market. I didn't know where I'd go or what I'd do, only that everything had to change. The stuff I didn't sell or donate I crammed into boxes. My spare room looked like a dead letter office.

I spent my days taking long drives, sitting in near-empty movie theaters, hiking back trails, napping in the woods. Whatever I did was meant to keep me from doing something else. From drinking vodka with breakfast. From lying in bed until my limbs quit working. From turning up on Cheryl's doorstep. I was stalling. A chapter that should have been over kept lingering on. I wanted closure. Somehow I knew it wouldn't be long. I'd even prepared for it.

I was getting home from a late-afternoon stroll around Lady Bird Lake when Cole made his final appearance. I found him sitting in the same striped recliner—one of the few pieces of furniture I still owned—and holding the same .358 on his lap. He'd grown a beard and shaved his head to the bone. His leather jacket lay crumpled at his feet. He nodded to me but didn't bother getting up. I wasn't startled. The truth is, I came back every day expecting him to be there.

He pointed to his jacket.

"I found the bug," he said. "I assume there were more in my car, but of course I had to ditch that."

"I figured," I said.

He smiled: there was no reason for either of us to deny anything anymore.

"Seems like you're on the move," he said, aiming the barrel of his gun at a column of boxes in the corner.

"And you're on the run," I said. "The new look suits you."

"Why don't you put your piece on the floor and slide it over here."

"I'm not carrying today."

"Bullshit."

I lifted up my T-shirt, turned in a slow circle.

"Well, I'll be damned," he said.

He balanced the gun on his thigh, pulled a cigar from his breast pocket, and lit it.

"Is there a reason I'm still alive?" I asked.

"I have no reason for you to be dead."

"So why are you here?"

"Pull up a box and have a seat," he said.

"Thanks, but I'd rather stand."

He grinned.

"This is a fund-raising visit," he said. "My accounts have been frozen. I need travel money."

"Coming to me is awfully risky. The cops already think I'm helping you."

"I'm aware, but I have something to sell. Something only you would buy."

"What's that?"

He reached forward, pulled his jacket from the floor like it was a magic cape, revealed a short stack of letter-sized envelopes.

"This is all of them," he said. "All of the missives poor Louis signed before his demise. The authorities might be less likely to believe in his suicide given recent events, but they'd have no trouble believing the rest. At the very least, they'd make your life unbearable."

"Isn't that your job?"

"I guess you could say I'm resigning."

I had no intention of paying, but I figured I'd play along until he showed his full hand.

"How much do you want?" I asked.

"I'm not unreasonable. I know cash isn't flowing for you now the way it once was. Let's say fifty thousand."

"I don't have anywhere near that," I said.

"How much can you manage?"

"Companion is closed. The condo hasn't sold. The best I can do is five grand."

He gave a theatrical double take.

"Those letters are worth your life," he said.

"You take credit cards? Otherwise, I can't spend what I don't have."

He sucked a long drag off his cigar, shrugged as he blew out smoke.

"I guess five grand will sound better once I convert it to pesos."

"The banks are closed now. I can get it for you tomorrow."

"I should be able to manage another day."

I knew then that the letters were a ruse, or maybe an icebreaker. There was something bigger on his mind.

"Why don't you tell me what you really want," I said.

He laughed.

"Sounds like you're imagining something sinister," he said. "What I really want is for you to cook me one last meal. A last supper, if you will."

"You're kidding."

"I'm not. You know I'm worthless in a kitchen, and I can't show my face—even my altered face—in public. It's been weeks since I had a decent meal, and I'm afraid the pickings will be slim where I'm headed."

"My fridge isn't exactly stocked right now."

"Not a problem—I took the liberty of stocking it. You'll find everything you need in a plastic bag on the top shelf. The pork chops should cook up quickly. I realize the lemon mousse won't have time to chill properly, but you take what you can get."

"All right," I said. "You're the one holding a gun."

He stood on the opposite side of the island, drinking my scotch and chain-smoking cigars while I rubbed the pork chops with salt, pepper, and dried sage, then sautéed them in canola oil. My stomach held steady: Prilosec helped as long as I kept to a few thousand fat-free calories per day. Cole said nothing, looked uncharacteristically sad and preoccupied, like he was writing his memoir in his head. I steamed a big pile of assorted vegetables, had the meal ready inside of twenty minutes. Cole ate at the counter while I prepared the mousse.

"Don't you want to eat with me?" he asked.

"I'm not hungry," I lied.

He took a bite, let out a staged moan.

"Do you remember Leon Ramos?" he asked.

"Of course. He taught cooking at the center. I must have taken a dozen classes with him."

"He's a chef now at the Plaza in New York."

"You kept tabs on him?"

"I thought he might prove useful. To you. You were the reason I hired him."

"Bullshit. His classes sold out in a heartbeat."

"Do you really think the head chef at Austin's top five-star restaurant wanted to teach at a rec center? I paid him ten times what I paid every other instructor."

I quit whisking the egg whites and sugar, and looked over at him. "Why?"

"Why do you think?"

"I mean, why tell me now?"

He speared a piece of broccoli with his fork, lifted it to his mouth, and then set it back down.

"My own son tried to kill me," he said. "He sat on his hate for all those years before he snapped. I need to know what broke him."

So he'd figured it out. The father-in-law must have played double agent. I waited for Cole to show his gun again, but he just stood there looking expectant.

"It could be anything," I said. "Maybe a song triggered his memory. Or maybe it was seeing you on TV."

He pressed on his eyes with the heels of his palms, held them there for a long beat.

"I haven't been the person I wanted to be," he said. "Somewhere along the way I lost track of who that person was. You're young enough still. Be vigilant. This life is more distraction than substance."

He swallowed the last of his pork chop.

"Delicious," he said. "Now, if you don't mind, I have to use the restroom."

"Down that hall," I said.

He was making it easy for me. Easier than it should have been. I waited until I heard the door shut behind him, then took a small and unmarked glass vial from the cabinet above the fridge. Tetrodotoxin, the puffer fish poison. I'd bought it off one of Ryan's old running buddies. I steadied my hands, slipped on a pair of latex gloves, pulled out the stopper, and emptied the contents into the mixing bowl. I finished whisking, then poured the mousse into a large ice cream sundae glass.

"Sorry for that little display," Cole said when he came back. "This is a stressful time."

"I can imagine," I said.

"I suppose you can."

I slid the glass over, handed him a dessert spoon.

"Looks wonderful," he said.

I thought my palms would be slick. I thought my voice would crack. But if I felt anything, it was resigned. Like this moment had been coming for a long while.

Cole let a heaping spoonful melt on his tongue.

"You know," he said, "I think I prefer it warm. Cold dulls the flavor."

He took another bite, then another. When he was done, he pushed the glass aside, covered a slight belch with his fist.

"My God, that was something," he said. "*Last Supper* may have been a front, but you did those inmates a real service."

He ran his fingers through his beard, pressed on his temples like something inside him was trying to break free.

"I'm feeling kind of light-headed," he said. "Come sit with me."

I followed him into the living room. He took his seat in the recliner, pushed back, and shut his eyes. There was a long beat before either of us spoke.

"I feel it now," he said. "How much time do I have?"

My pulse spiked.

"Feel what?"

He sniggered.

"Don't be an ass. Why do you think I came here? If all I wanted was money, the gun would have sufficed. I know you were tracking me. The old man must have talked."

He was shivering now. His bare scalp had gone slick with sweat.

"Yeah," I said. "He did."

"So how long do I have?"

"Not long."

"Good. You set Roger up, but I drove you to it. I know I did."

His voice was garbled with phlegm. I pulled a small blanket from the back of the recliner, held it out to him. He waved me off, forced a little smile.

"Water," he said. "Cold."

I stepped into the kitchen, filled a glass with ice, and topped it off with tap water. I thought lemon might be more than he could handle. When I came back, he had his phone on his lap and was typing with his thumbs.

"A last goodbye," he said, taking the glass. "Believe it or not, I have friends."

"I'm sure you do," I said.

I watched him struggle to force down a sip of water. I wasn't scared. I didn't wish like hell that I could take it back. I was only anxious for the end.

"You would have liked Roger," he said. "The two of you—"

He grabbed at his gut, lunged forward, vomited out food and blood and white foam. I turned away, heard him drop to the floor behind me.

"Thank you," he whispered.

As though I'd done his bidding, even at the end.

"You're welcome," I said.

And then I collapsed on the floor beside him. I couldn't bring myself to hate him just then, any more than I could explain why I was crying. I took his hand. I thought of something Slither said during our interview: *Your own death's all you got left in this world, so you want it to last.* I felt for a pulse, but he was already gone.

I sat there for a long while, not looking at him, not really looking at anything. At first my mind shot around too fast to land on a single thought, and then it went blank.

Get up, I told myself. *Move.*

On my way to the bathroom, I kicked something hard and heard it go skidding across the floor. Cole's cell phone. I'd forgotten all about his final goodbye.

The last message he sent was just two words long: *Do it.*

Delivered to Ron HV thirty-five minutes ago. Read ten minutes ago.

HV could only stand for *Huntsville.*

Ron was the name of Ryan's CO.

CHAPTER 31

I couldn't get ahold of Ottie. I called and hung up and called and hung up and called and hung up. I left a message, then called and hung up again. I sent a half dozen texts and stood staring at the screen, waiting for it to light up. Nothing. I grabbed my car keys and ran. Let Cole and his mess lie there for now.

I didn't know what I'd do once I got to Huntsville—I only knew that I couldn't be here. It was Friday night and the traffic was heavy leaving Austin. I kept one hand hovering above the horn. I cranked the AC as high as it would go, but the sweat kept coming.

"All right," I said out loud. "Calm the fuck down."

I tried to talk myself into a better place. Maybe I had more time than I thought. Ron HV would have to play it careful. He couldn't just waltz into Ryan's cell and slit his throat. He'd have to wait for the dead of night, when the inmates were asleep and the guards were lazy about their rounds. I looked at the dashboard clock. It was just 9:00 p.m. I had a chance. I'd kick and scream and do whatever it took to get eyes on my brother. I'd set fire to myself if I had to.

Past the city limits, the traffic thinned, and about twenty miles farther out, I got the fast lane to myself. I watched the speedometer tip past a hundred miles per hour. If a trooper pulled me over, I'd give him a shined-up version of the truth. I had a brother in Huntsville, and someone I didn't know had called to say he wouldn't live through the night. The trooper would have to radio ahead just to cover his own ass. And then whoever answered would have to do the same. Ron would be forced to back off. At least for the night.

I was fifty miles out when my phone broke into the chorus of "Prisoner of Love." I snatched it from the cup holder, started talking before she knew I was on the line.

"Listen, Ottie," I said. "You've got to pull Ryan from his cell. Now."

"James—"

"Please, Ottie. He's in danger. He's going to get hurt. It's going to happen tonight. I know that sounds—"

"James, there's something I have to—"

"Just listen to me. There isn't time. Get him out of there, and I'll explain—"

"You're too late, James."

She shouted it the way people shout when the person they're talking to is hysterical. It worked. She didn't have to say another thing. I swerved through the slow lane and came to a screeching stop on the shoulder.

"What do you mean?" I asked.

"Are you sure you want me to—"

"What happened?"

She blurted it out like she was afraid of losing steam.

"He killed himself, James," she said.

"How?"

"He cut his wrists."

"With what?"

"He sharpened the end of a toothbrush."

"That's bullshit."

"I'm sorry, James, but—"

"He didn't kill himself. Someone—"

"Listen, we checked the video. It was the first thing we did. No one else came in or out of his cell."

"Ryan didn't kill himself."

Now I was shouting. I couldn't help myself. I sounded like an overtired child fighting for a later bedtime.

"I know this is hard," she said, "but—"

"He had his appeal next week. Cheryl . . . his lawyer said he had a good chance."

"Maybe that's why. Getting off death row would have meant life in prison. Some people can't face that."

"Ryan could."

I didn't know where to go from there. I couldn't finger Ron HV without mentioning the dead man lying on my living room floor. I couldn't share that two-word text without explaining why I had Cole's phone.

"James?"

"I want to see him."

"Now?"

"I'm already in the car."

"But you can't. His cell is still a crime scene. It'll be hours, maybe longer, before—"

"I'll wait."

"That's not a good idea."

"Why not?"

"Do you have someone you can be with?"

"I want to be with my brother."

"That's not possible."

"Why? What's going on?"

She took a deep breath. I knew I wouldn't like whatever came out on the other side.

"I can't give you the same privileges as before, James."

"What are you talking about? This is the end, Ottie. I won't have anything to ask for after this."

"It isn't that. It's . . ."

"What?"

"You know, James."

"I don't."

"Really? *Last Supper* was supposed to boost Huntsville's image, and it ended with two people murdered in your restaurant. That falls on my shoulders. I can't be seen—"

"Fuck you, Ottie," I said, and hung up.

But of course she was right. I'd made her life harder, and she didn't owe me a thing.

I pulled back onto the highway, reversed direction, and drove at a snail's pace, like it was the car thinking instead of me. I tried to line up my best memories, but it was too soon for that. Instead I found myself worrying about the practical shit. The burial. The where and the when and the who of it. The flowers and the stone and the preacher. I dug so deep into the details that I almost forgot there was someone else I had to bury first.

CHAPTER 32

I told myself I'd wait until after the funeral, but that was more than I could manage. The stupid fucker wasn't hard to track down. I took his number from Cole's phone, did a reverse search, and voilà. It dawned on me that he didn't know Cole was dead, that I could text him and have him meet me somewhere, but then I'd be inviting all kinds of problems. When a bad man disappears, his accomplices want him to stay disappeared. Ron HV might show up at a rendezvous with a CO sharpshooter on standby. Or he might assume Cole was summoning him to his death and take off.

In the end, I kept it simple. I came up on him while he was mowing his lawn in the middle of a balmy Sunday afternoon.

"Hey there, Ron," I called.

That was all he needed. He looked over, saw who I was, then turned and ran. I had him by the throat before he reached his front door.

"Get the fuck off me," he yelped.

I threw him backward onto the pebbled walkway, pinned him down, started pummeling. I'd had a whole sermon prepared, but there didn't seem to be any point: he knew why I was there. He threw up his hands but couldn't think of what to do beyond that. I hit him on the side of the head, in the chest and arms, then square on the jaw. His hands dropped and his eyes spun around, but he was still conscious.

"I didn't kill him," he said.

His lips and teeth were all blood.

"Nice try."

I split his cheek open with a right cross.

"I gave him the shank. That's all."

"Bullshit."

"I swear to God."

I pummeled him some more. He was fading now, winking out like a near-dead star. I put my hands back around his throat. He didn't have the strength to resist. I started counting inside my head like I wanted to see how long it would take. I didn't bother to look around. I didn't care if anyone was watching. *Four, five ...*

I couldn't do it.

I jumped up like my legs were springs, started pacing the grass, cursing and spitting.

"I'm sorry," he gurgled.

Beneath all the blood and spit he was sobbing.

"You're a fucking piece of shit," I said.

I stepped over him, stood straddling his torso. Almost without knowing I would, I reached into my pocket, pulled out my phone, and snapped his picture.

"That's to remind myself what I'm capable of," I told him.

If he heard me at all, he must have thought I was talking about the beating. But that wasn't it. I wanted something I could look at any time I needed to remember that I'd stopped myself. A note to the future me saying, *This is also who you are.*

•

We buried Ryan on a crisp day, under a pure blue sky. There wasn't much of a crowd: just me, Cheryl, Ottie, and the preacher. I was Ryan's only family, and he didn't have friends—at least none that stuck by him once he was locked up. Ottie came straight at me with a hug, and neither of us mentioned her banning me from Huntsville.

Cheryl smiled and took my hand. I tried not to think about how she looked in her black skirt suit.

Cemetery workers lowered the casket into a plot beside our mother and father, two people who, in the end, we didn't really know. Then the priest said some words I doubt anyone heard. Inside, I was burning with regret over the fact that Ryan's death would go down a suicide. Like that was the greatest injustice of his life. And the biggest disgrace. Not the drugs or the armed robbery or the murder. I didn't want people thinking he'd given up on himself. Or maybe I didn't want them thinking I couldn't help my own brother.

Afterward, Cheryl sat with me in a café across from the cemetery. I drank mint tea and she ate a slice of key lime pie. She didn't say "sorry for your loss" or "he's in a better place" or any of the usual bullshit. For a while, neither of us spoke at all. Cheryl just kind of looked at her hands while I stared out the window.

Then she said, "You know, at first I blamed you."

"Blamed me?"

She nodded.

"You put me in a situation. I tried, but I couldn't stop wanting to protect you. If I'd gone to the police, recused myself, accepted whatever punishment the bar handed down . . . If I'd been willing to see you in a jumpsuit . . ."

"For what?" I said. "If Ryan hadn't killed someone, I never would have—"

"That's too easy," she said. "On the surface it's true. On the surface it makes perfect sense. But dig a little deeper and you have to see that it's just too easy."

She was right, but I was still angry. Maybe I was angry because she was right. Maybe my anger had nothing to do with her.

"Listen, I just buried my brother. I—"

"I know," she said. "I'm not done. I said I blamed you at first. And myself, too. I guess as Ryan's lawyer, I still blame myself. But that isn't fair to Ryan. It doesn't honor his choice. If he decided there was no working with the hand he'd been dealt, then we—the left behind—have to accept that."

She'd taken at face value something I still couldn't believe: that Ryan really had killed himself. Maybe I'd believe it someday, but not now. In any case, she had a point. Ryan had lived a life. He'd had a few shining moments and a whole lot of fuckups. He'd done things, and things had been done to him. But a book is more than its last chapter, and Ryan wasn't just a tragic ending. That couldn't be how I remembered him.

"What about you?" she asked. "What's next?"

I shrugged.

"You have a clean slate now," she said. "Or at least a new beginning. I know that sounds cold, but it's true."

I couldn't admit I'd had the same thought.

"So what are you going to do with yourself?" she asked.

"I haven't really thought about it."

"Of course you have," she said. "That isn't bad. It's just human nature."

"There's someone I might contact in New York. A chef. He used to live here. I took some classes with him."

I said it just to say something. The truth was, I didn't have so much as a direction to turn in.

"Is that what you want?"

I couldn't help it. I thought, *You're what I want, Cheryl.* But all I said was, "I guess I can't know till I'm there."

"I mean cooking," she said. "Being a chef. Is that still what you want?"

I remembered all over again why Cheryl was born to be a lawyer: she had a gift for cutting through the fat and finding the question you least wanted to answer.

"It used to be everything," I said. "Now . . ."

"Now what?"

"I don't know. I try to think about it, but any time I get close, my mind turns away."

She nodded like I'd said something profound.

"How's your stomach these days?" she asked.

"Better," I said.

Which was true. The drugs were working. I hadn't been sick since the night Ryan died.

"Then do me a favor," she said. "Shut your eyes."

"Cheryl, I—"

"Just humor me."

I obeyed.

"Now open your mouth," she said.

I felt metal against my tongue and then by instinct my mouth closed and she slid the spoon back and I could taste cold and sweet and bitter at once.

"What do you think?" she asked.

"Very nice," I said.

"But you'd know how to make it great?"

She smiled. It was true: my mind was churning out a list of corrections. Ease up on the lime zest. Replace the egg yolks with sour cream.

"Spend some time mourning," Cheryl said. "And then, whatever you do, don't compromise. And I'm not talking about money or fame."

She stood, slid what was left of her pie in front of me, and kissed my cheek.

"It's all yours," she said.

I watched her cross the street, get into her car, and drive off.

There was a family entering the cemetery on foot through the main gates: mother, father, and daughter. They weren't dressed in black like they were going to a funeral, but they weren't wearing jeans and flip-flops, either. They looked worn-out, as if they'd walked a long way just to get here. The mother seemed to favor her left leg; the father carried a bouquet of flowers carelessly in one hand, so that their bulbs almost scraped the ground. The girl, who couldn't have been more than ten or eleven, hung her head like she didn't understand and wanted to be off skating in the park or playing with her friends.

As a family, they didn't seem to like one another very much. I imagined they were going to visit a relative only one of them had really known. The mother's mother, I decided. Father and daughter were tagging along out of obligation. Somehow, you could tell these weekly trips had become the centerpiece of whatever was pulling the family apart. Maybe they were having money problems. Maybe the mother had been offered a job in another city and the father didn't want to go. Resentments built up over the years, and there wasn't enough love left to support a move. Of course the girl sensed this, and deep down she believed it must be her fault. Sometimes she felt crippled by guilt, while other times she just wanted to be away from it all—far, far away, living someone else's life.

I took another bite of Cheryl's pie and watched them climb the steep hill between the gates and the cemetery's first headstone. The flavor of the pie mixed with their image, and I caught myself planning a meal for them, struggling to find something they would all enjoy, even if each of them enjoyed it for different reasons. Something flavorful. Something that would hold them sitting in the same place for as long as it took to finish every last bite. A Moroccan chicken, maybe. Too tame to offend suburban taste buds, but exotic enough to stir vague fantasies of foreign lands. I saw the dish laid out on the table with the family gathered around, and I believed that soon they would be talking, and that the talking would lead to laughter. And then, as they talked and laughed over the meal I'd prepared, they would remember that they had one another's backs, that they were a family, and whatever happened to one of them would happen to all of them. And as they crested that hill and disappeared from sight, I thought, *No, I promise, I will never compromise again.*